Her job was wonderful, better than she'd ever imagined, but what kept her up at nights wasn't her job.

It was Keir.

She wanted him. In her arms. In her bed, and to hell with whether or not he'd respect her in the morning. She already knew the answer. He wouldn't…but she didn't care anymore. She wanted Keir, wanted him, wanted him—

"You know what you need, Berk?" he said softly.

Her mouth was as dry as the Nevada desert. "Do you?"

"Yes." His voice roughened, and she could feel her heart trying to leap from her breast.

"You need a lesson, and I'm the man to give it to you."

"Keir…" His name came out a whisper. "Keir…"

"What time does lunch finish up?"

She blinked. Sex by appointment? "Four, but why do you—"

"Good." He turned away. "Be ready to go at five-thirty."

Dear Reader,

Welcome to the exciting, passion-filled world of the O'Connells. Meet Keir, the eldest O'Connell son, and Cassie, a young woman whom life has sometimes treated unkindly. Cassie's worked at Keir's hotel, but he never really noticed her. Now, in the first book in the O'Connell series, Keir lets us in on a secret. He can't forget what happened between him and Cassie one magical night under a hot summer moon. Cassie can't forget, either...and that's when the fireworks begin.

You've told me how much you loved the Barons. I hope you'll show that same generous warmth to the O'Connells. Please take Keir, Sean, Cullen, Fallon, Megan and Briana into your hearts. Then come along with me and their proud, powerful mother, Mary Elizabeth O'Connell Coyle, as we begin that most important of life's journeys—a search for deep, passionate, all-enduring love.

With love,

Sandra Marton

You can e-mail Sandra at: www.sandramarton.com

Sandra Marton

KEIR O'CONNELL'S MISTRESS

The O'CONNELLS

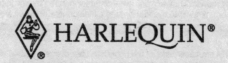

HARLEQUIN®

TORONTO • NEW YORK • LONDON
AMSTERDAM • PARIS • SYDNEY • HAMBURG
STOCKHOLM • ATHENS • TOKYO • MILAN • MADRID
PRAGUE • WARSAW • BUDAPEST • AUCKLAND

ISBN 0-373-12309-4

KEIR O'CONNELL'S MISTRESS

First North American Publication 2003.

Visit us at www.eHarlequin.com

Printed in U.S.A.

CHAPTER ONE

Late summer, on the road to Las Vegas:

THE sun was a hint of gold lighting the rim of the desert as Keir O'Connell crossed the state line into Nevada.

The road was empty and he was driving fast, the black Ferrari eating up the miles like the powerful thoroughbred it was. A sign flashed by, so quickly Keir couldn't read it, but he didn't have to. He knew what it said.

75 miles to Las Vegas. Welcome to the Desert Song Hotel and Casino.

Seventy-five miles. At the speed he was driving, little more than half an hour away.

Keir eased back on the gas pedal.

He'd been on the road for two days, driving almost non-stop, knowing he'd pushed things too far and if he didn't hurry, he'd miss his mother's wedding.

The thought was almost enough to make him smile.

Missing the duchess's wedding wasn't an option. She'd wait until all six of her children were gathered before taking her vows with Dan Coyle. Afterward, she'd peel the hide off whichever of them had caused the delay.

No, missing the wedding wasn't a possibility. Besides— Keir checked the dashboard clock—besides, he'd make it in plenty of time. The ceremony wasn't until tomorrow. He'd told himself he was driving hard because he wanted the chance to visit with his family and that was part of it, yes, but the greater truth was that driving fast relaxed him.

He knew, from long experience, that taking a car almost to its limit, seeing how far he could push the speed until he was hovering on that razor-sharp edge between control and the loss of it, was usually enough to drain him of tension. That, or being with a woman, but that was the last thing he wanted now.

He hadn't touched a woman in the thirty days he'd been gone...in the month since he'd made an ass of himself in a moonlit Texas garden with Cassie Berk.

One month. Was that all the time he'd been away? Had he really made so many life-altering decisions in four short weeks? It didn't seem possible, especially for him. He'd spent a lifetime with his brothers teasing him about being such a vigilant planner.

"Be careful," his mother had said the year he'd gotten his pilot's license, and one of his brothers—Sean, maybe—had laughed and hugged her and said there was no reason to worry, that Keir would never have an accident unless he planned it first.

Keir frowned.

Then, how come he was about to sign off as Chief Operating Officer of the Desert Song and move twenty-five hundred miles across the country to a vineyard in Connecticut—a vineyard into which he'd sunk a small fortune?

Keir shifted in his seat and tried to find a better angle for his legs. The Ferrari had more room under the dashboard than some cars he'd driven but it was built for speed, not comfort, especially if you topped six foot two.

What he was going to do would make anyone edgy. And, yeah, why lie to himself? The prospect of seeing Cassie again bothered him, too. It bothered him a lot. Nobody went through life without doing something stupid; despite what Cassie had called him, he wasn't arrogant enough to think he was the exception to the rule. But what he'd done that night...

He owed her an apology. She'd be calmer by now, willing to let him eat crow and say he was sorry he'd come on to her. It had been the mood and the moment, that was all. Too much champagne, too much slow dancing, too much of the enforced togetherness that came of him being Gray

Baron's best man and Cassie being Dawn Lincoln's maid of honor.

It was his fault, all of it, and he was prepared to admit it. He was her boss, dammit; he knew the rules about sexual harassment. Knew them? He'd *written* them at the Song, not just rules about harassment but others that clearly laid out what he expected of people.

Logic. Reason. Common sense. He believed in those principles. He'd built his life on them…and forgotten every last one, that night with Cassie.

"You're an arrogant, self-centered, stupid son of a bitch," she'd said, breathing fire when he'd done the right thing, stepped back and tried to say he was sorry.

Had she let him? No way. She'd rounded on him with fury and the worst of it was that the things she'd called him might have dented his ego, but they were true.

He'd made a move on her he never should have made and put her in the position where she'd been damned if she responded and damned if she didn't.

She'd responded, all right.

He'd taken her in his arms in a dark corner of the garden at that Texas ranch. A second later, she'd been clinging to him, opening her mouth to his, moaning as he'd bunched up her skirt and slid his hands under her dress, that long, gauzy dress that made her look like an old-fashioned dream instead of a Las Vegas cocktail waitress…

This kind of crap wasn't going to get him anywhere. He was maybe fifty miles from Vegas and exactly thirty days and nights from what had happened—what had almost happened—in that garden, and why was he thinking about it again?

He was hungry, that was why. His stomach wasn't just growling, it was snarling. He'd pretty much been living on black coffee and catnaps, just pulling off the road long enough to fill the car with gas and his system with caffeine. It had been a long forty-eight hours from Connecticut to Nevada.

If you wanted to get philosophical, he thought, goosing the car back to speed, it had been the longest journey of his life.

Other cars were feeding onto the road now, all of them heading toward that glittering Mecca in the desert. Keir slowed the Ferrari to what seemed a crawl.

He'd gone to New York on vacation, though that hadn't been his original plan. He'd intended to drive to Tucson, then to Phoenix, just get away for a couple of weeks, enjoy the feel of the car—he'd bought it only weeks before—on the long, straight desert roads.

And then, right after the ceremony, his mother and Dan Coyle, the Desert Song's Head of Security, had taken him aside.

"Keir," the duchess had said, clinging to Dan Coyle's arm, "I know this will come as a surprise...darling, Dan and I are getting married."

Keir smiled.

A surprise? Yeah, but once he'd thought about it, he realized it shouldn't have been. He'd caught Dan casting longing looks at the duchess for quite a while and caught her blushing like a schoolgirl in response.

So he'd kissed his mother, clapped Dan on the back, and after they'd laughed and maybe cried a little, the duchess had taken his hands in hers and told him that he was to take a month's holiday, at least.

"Orders from on high must be obeyed," Dan had said with a wink, when Keir had begun to protest.

"You deserve a real vacation," Mary had insisted. "Just be sure you're back for the wedding."

Dan had grinned, told him that they'd chosen a date, even a time, and then Keir had kissed his mother, shaken Dan's hand, said if he expected him to start calling him Daddy he was in for a rude surprise.

And when all the good wishes and jokes were over, Keir had taken a deep breath and said he thought it might be time for Mary to take over the management of the Desert Song again, and for him to move on.

Dan had urged him to reconsider.

"Is it because I'm marrying your mother? Keir, that isn't necessary. There's no need for you to leave."

"No," Mary had said softly, "of course there isn't." Her smile had trembled a little. "But he wants to leave. Don't you, Keir? Running the Song was never what you wanted to do in the first place." She'd touched his arm. "I think I've always known that."

It was the truth and Keir hadn't denied it. They'd talked a bit, the three of them, of how things would be with him gone and Mary in charge.

"With Dan sharing responsibility," she'd said firmly and Keir had nodded his agreement. He liked Coyle; he'd be good for the duchess and if anyone could keep her in line, Keir figured Dan could.

After that, he'd gone back to the wedding festivities...

And Cassie.

Keir frowned, took his sunglasses from the visor and slipped them on.

He'd intended to start for Tucson early the next morning but after the fiasco in the garden, he'd tossed his things in his car and headed east instead of west, not just in search of a holiday but in search of his own life.

It was one thing to be free of the responsibilities he'd assumed six years ago, but free to do what? The only thing he was sure of was that he didn't want to go back to arbitrage. He'd made a fortune in the complex world of stocks and bonds before taking over the Song, but that was the past.

He had yet to glimpse the future.

To that end, and, yeah, maybe because he'd figured that keeping busy would block memories of how stupidly he'd behaved with Cassie, he'd made some discreet inquiries of colleagues once he reached New York. Within a couple of days, an attorney representing a French hotel conglomerate

approached him about a five star facility planned for the
East side of Manhattan. They wanted his expertise and were
willing to pay handsomely for it. A lunch, then a couple of
dinners, and Keir had begun thinking about becoming a
consultant in New York. The idea pleased him. He loved
the pace and power of the city and started looking to put
down roots.

That was why he'd been standing on the terrace of a
penthouse a few mornings ago, the realtor beside him gush-
ing over the view, the rooms, the lap pool and spa, when
suddenly her voice seemed to fade and Keir had found himself seeing not the view but himself, forever trapped inside
a paneled office, forever doomed to wear a suit and a tie
and sit behind a desk.

What had happened to the boy who'd wanted to be an
astronaut? To the kid who'd wanted to slay dragons? A
penthouse suite, a private pool and an expensive view had
never been part of those dreams.

How could he have forgotten that?

He'd turned to the realtor, told her he was sorry but he'd
just remembered an appointment. Then he'd gotten into the
Ferrari, pointed it north and let the car eat up the miles until
he'd found himself in Connecticut farmland.

He'd been driving without an agenda, figuring on turning
back once he knew what in hell he was doing, but the
weather was beautiful the car was purring. When he pulled
out a map while he filled up at a gas station, he realized
that if he went just another few miles he could check out
the Song's competition. A couple of northeastern Native
American tribes had opened casinos and hotels in
Connecticut. They were very successful. Why not combine
business with pleasure and take a look? He might not be
running the Song anymore, but he might find something
interesting to pass on to Dan and his mother.

So Keir had piled back into his car and headed a little
further north and east.

The Native American casinos had proved enlightening.

He'd spent the rest of the morning strolling around, discreetly observing the operations. Then for reasons he'd never be able to fathom, he'd gotten back in the Ferrari and driven another hour, hour and a half, until he'd ended up on a road that knifed through tall stands of oak and maple, where his car was the only traffic and the only sound was the cry of a hawk, circling overhead.

He'd almost missed the sign.

DEER RUN VINEYARD, it read, *Luncheon and Dinner Thursday thru Sunday, By Reservation Only.*

It was Thursday, Keir had thought, glancing at his watch. It was almost two. A little late for lunch and besides, you needed a reservation but, what the hell?

So he'd turned down a narrow dirt road and found, at its end, a scene that might have been a painting: a handsome old barn converted into a small restaurant, a garden surrounding a patio filled with umbrella tables and a profusion of flowers, and beyond that, row after row of grapevines climbing a hill toward a handsome old stone house set against a cloudless blue sky.

Keir felt a tightening in his belly.

Yes, the hostess said, someone had just phoned to cancel a reservation for the second seating. If he'd just wait a few minutes...?

He'd accepted a glass of wine and gone for a stroll up the hill, walking through the rows of vines, drawing the rich smell of the earth and the grapes deep into his lungs...

And suddenly known that he belonged here.

He'd asked the owner to join him for coffee. Keir came straight to the point. He wanted to buy Deer Run. The proprietor beamed. His wife was ill; she needed a change of climate. They'd decided to put the place up for sale just days before. What a nice surprise, that Keir should have turned up wanting to buy it.

Keir hadn't been surprised. Until that afternoon he'd never believed in anything a man couldn't see or touch but something—he didn't want to call it fate—*something* had been at work that day.

He'd looked at the books, had data faxed to his accountant and attorney. Before the sun dipped behind the gently rolling hills, he'd become the new owner of Deer Run.

Stupid? His accountant and attorney were too polite to say so. What they *did* say was "impulsive."

Keir speeded up a little and changed lanes. Maybe they were right, but he had no regrets. He needed to change his life, and now he'd done it.

Las Vegas, ten miles.

The sign flashed by before he knew it—before he was ready. He slowed the car to a crawl.

He was not a man who ever acted on impulse and yet he'd done so three times in the past few weeks, walking out on the French deal, buying a winery...kissing a woman he shouldn't have kissed.

Why regret any of it?

The kiss was just a kiss, the five star hotel and the penthouse in New York had been wrong for him, but the winery...the winery felt right.

No, he thought, he had no regrets at all. Not even about Cassie.

Keir turned on the radio and heard the pulse of hard, pounding rock. One thing he'd learned during this trip was you could tell where you were by listening to local DJ's. Back east there'd been lots of Dylan and Debussy. The closer he'd come to the middle of the country, the more he'd heard Garth Brooks. Now, with the desert behind him and the Vegas strip just ahead, the sounds of rock and roll were kicking in.

Actually, what he liked best were the old standards, the stuff nobody played anymore. He'd grown up listening to those songs, *Embraceable You* and *Starlight* and the rest; his parents had always seen to it that music like that was featured in at least one lounge at the Desert Song.

The band had played lots of those numbers at Gray and

Dawn's wedding, especially as evening came on. He'd been dancing with Cassie, the two of them laughing as they moved to something by the Stones, when suddenly the music had become slow and smoky.

That was when he'd gathered her into his arms, as if the whole day had been leading up to that moment.

He knew the reasons.

People did things they'd never think of doing when they went to weddings and parties where the wine flowed and inhibitions got tossed aside.

How many toasts had he drunk? How many dances had he danced with Cassie, watching the flash of her long legs, the way her dress clung to her body when the summer breeze blew? How often had he inhaled her scent when he leaned close to ask if she wanted something from the buffet?

Why wouldn't she have suddenly seemed a beautiful, mysterious creature of every man's hottest dreams instead of a woman who might have been around the block more times than he wanted to count?

As he'd danced her into the garden, away from the lights, away from the other guests, he'd even imagined asking her to go with him the next day. He'd thought of what it might be like to be alone with her in some quiet, romantic hideaway.

"Cassie," he'd murmured, tilting her face to his in the darkness. And he'd kissed her. Just kissed her...

Until she made a little sound, moved against him and dammit suddenly, his hands had been all over her, molding her to him, lifting her into him, sliding under her skirt against soft, silken skin.

Keir tightened his grip on the steering wheel.

Great. He was right back where he'd been when he'd pointed his car east the night of the wedding, feeling like a damned fool for having hit on a woman who worked for him, who'd probably been afraid to say "no" or maybe figured making it with the boss would improve her chances of being something better than a cocktail waitress...

He could still feel the way she'd stiffened in his arms, hear the sound of her voice.

"Keir," she'd said, "Keir, no."

That was what had brought him back to sanity, the way she'd said his name, her voice shaking, her body losing its soft, warm pliancy—and maybe that had been part of the act, a game designed to make him want her all the more—except, if he'd wanted her any more, he'd have exploded.

Keir cursed, stepped on the brakes and brought the car to a skidding stop on the side of the road.

Okay. He'd made a fool of himself but he'd done that before and survived. Not with a woman. Never with a woman, but he'd done his fair share of dumb things. Like making cold phone calls as a trainee at a San Francisco brokerage house and being set up by one of the other trainees so that somehow he'd ended up phoning the wife of the firm's CEO.

He'd sold her three hundred shares of stock.

Now there was Cassie. Well, yeah. He was sorry he'd kissed her, but seeing her again, apologizing, wasn't going to be any problem at all. Wasn't there some old Irish saying about a little humility lightening the load and being good for the soul?

If there wasn't, there ought to be.

As for buying the vineyard... Keir took a deep breath and pulled the car back into traffic. Enough introspection. He was minutes from home, his mother was getting married tomorrow, and he had the feeling he was in for one hell of an old-fashioned, rowdy O'Connell family reunion.

Up ahead, a creature that looked like a small, slow-moving tank stepped out of the scrub. It looked from side to side, took a cautious step forward, then an equally cautious step back.

Keir braked, swung wide, and left the armadillo in the dust.

* * *

Half an hour later, he pulled into the employee lot at the Desert Song and parked his car in its usual space. The security guard at the back entrance gave him a big smile.

"Hey, Mr. O'Connell. You're back."

"How're you doing, Howard?" Keir stuck out his hand. "How's your wife? That baby's due any time now, isn't it?"

"Yes, sir. Couple of weeks. How was the vacation?"

"Terrific."

"And now it's back to work, huh?"

"Something like that." Keir clapped the guard on the shoulder. "Take care, Howard. Be sure and let me add my good wishes when the baby gets here."

Keir stopped smiling as he stepped inside the hotel and walked down the hall that led past a series of offices. He could almost feel the place swallow him up. Even dragging a breath into his lungs seemed difficult.

A month away, and now he really knew how much he wanted out.

He stabbed the freight elevator call button, tucked his hands into the pockets of his well-worn Levi's and tipped back a little on his heels.

The duchess had made it clear that she'd understand, if he left the Song.

Would she, really?

He'd come to Vegas to help run the place after his father's death. He was the eldest son, the O'Connell offspring who'd proven himself Responsible with a capital R. Cullen wasn't. He'd just left college, a dozen credits short of his degree, to do God only knew what. Sean had been—well, nobody had been quite sure of what Sean had been doing or where he'd been doing it. And the girls—Megan, Fallon and Briana—had all still been away at school.

"You'll just stay for a bit," his mother had said, "only until I can handle things on my own."

After a year, he'd suggested they hire a Chief Operating Officer.

"I don't know that I'd feel comfortable with someone outside the family," Mary had told him. "Can you stay on a little longer, Keir?"

He had, and just when it looked as if his mother was ready to take the reins, she'd had a massive heart attack.

Keir pressed the call button again and made a mental note to have Maintenance check the elevators. There were only two cars in this bank and they got heavy use from employees. One, at least, should have been moving.

Now, by a twist of fate, he was free of the responsibility of the Song. Thanks to another twist, maybe he'd found what he'd been looking for, even if all he knew about wine was how to drink it.

Better not to think like that. Whatever he knew or didn't know about grapes and wine, he was glad he'd bought Deer Run, glad he was finally getting on with his life. He felt as if it had been on hold for years, not just the six he'd spent working for his mother but the years he'd spent taking university courses that bored him.

He'd never let himself think about that while he was in school or even afterward, but during the trip east, the car eating up the miles, he'd felt something pushing for acknowledgment inside him, as if what had gone on in that garden had only been the first step toward acceptance of the truth.

He was restless.

He'd *always* been restless, though he'd fought against it. He'd kept it hidden like a dirty secret, even from his family.

"My strong, dependable boy," his mother had told him once. "You're just like my Ruarch."

Dependable? His father? Ruarch O'Connell had been a gambler, shifting them all from place to place on the turn of a card and never giving a damn for a plan that stretched further than tomorrow.

The last thing he wanted was to be like his father. Keir believed in laying things out so you knew what was coming next. And he'd never so much as fed a coin into a slot machine in his entire life.

So, why was he gambling now?

He tightened his jaw and pressed the call button again.

Investing in a property wasn't gambling. It was logical. Reasonable. As reasonable as knowing, *knowing,* dammit, a woman wanted you and then letting her pretend she didn't…

He cursed under his breath, pounded a fist on the call button and glared at the light panel above the door.

What he needed was a shower, a quick nap and a meal. Then he'd have his head together. That was why he was going to his suite the back way, so he didn't run into the duchess or any of his brothers or sisters, who were probably at the Song by now.

He certainly wasn't going the back way to avoid seeing Cassie.

Funny, how he'd never much noticed her until that night in the garden. She was an employee. He probably wouldn't have known her name if she hadn't been Dawn's friend— and the duchess had taken an interest in Dawn.

Hello, Cassie.

Goodbye, Cassie.

That had been the extent of his involvement with her. He didn't even know how long she'd been working at the Song, just that she was there, serving free drinks in the casino, dressed in what he thought of as the casino uniform. A short black skirt topped by a low-cut blouse. Black fishnet stockings. High heels. Vegas was a town where scantily dressed women were the status quo. Why *would* he have noticed?

But she hadn't looked like that in Texas. Maybe that was the reason he'd become aware of her. Okay, maybe he had noticed her once or twice before. Even in a town like this, where beautiful women were a dime a dozen, Cassie's looks were special.

She'd gone into the night with him, let him touch her and kiss her, and then she'd said "no." Why? She'd been as turned-on as he, as eager for what should have come next...

Keir's mouth tightened.

Maybe she'd expected him to ignore that breathless little "no." Maybe she'd expected him to offer her something to sweeten the deal. Whatever the reason, it was a damned good thing she'd decided to stop him. He'd been lucky to get out in time.

What was it his brother Sean had once said about men and hot-looking women? Maybe it was Cullen who'd said it. Not that it mattered. The message was what counted.

Men suffered from ZTS. Zipper Think Syndrome, meaning when it came to sex, guys thought with their zippers instead of their heads.

Keir grinned. Yeah, that was it. The old ZTS theory.

The light above the elevator was moving at last. Twelve. Ten. Eight. Six. Two. Keir gave a relieved sigh as the car announced its arrival with a soft ping.

Okay. One problem solved. For all he cared, the doors could slide open, the Berk babe could be standing there with nothing on but her skin and it wouldn't mean a damn.

Except, that wasn't quite the scene. Cassie was inside the elevator, all right, wearing that little skirt, the clingy top, the high-heeled shoes...

Correction. She had only one shoe on. She was bent over the other one, which seemed to be stuck to the floor, her cute little bottom pointed straight at him. Either she was too busy to know she had an audience or she just didn't care.

And he was having trouble remembering that he was too old to be led astray by ZTS.

Man, he'd been on the road too long.

Keir cleared his throat and donned what he figured was his best Chief of Ops polite smile.

"Hello, Cassie."

She jolted upright and swiveled toward him, the look on

her face going quickly from surprise to recognition to displeasure.

"You!"

She filled the word with loathing. Well, he could hardly blame her. Her memories of the last time they'd met probably were no better than his. Be pleasant, he told himself. After all, he owed the lady an apology.

"Yeah, that's right. Me." Keir nodded at the shoe. "Having a problem?"

"No," she snapped, "I always stand around like this, with one shoe on and one shoe—"

The car began to move. She hadn't expected it and she jerked back.

"Careful!"

Keir grabbed for her but Cassie flung out a hand and caught the railing.

"Don't touch me!"

So much for being polite. "No problem. You want to break your neck, be my guest."

"I'm doing just fine on my own."

"Oh, yeah. I can see that." He watched, arms folded, as she tried to pull the shoe free again. "Stop being foolish, Berk. Let me help—or would you rather I put in a call to Maintenance and have them send up a work crew?"

"What? Those idiots? They're the ones who left this damned piece of wood here in the first place." She leaned down again. "I'll fix it myself."

Maybe. But he couldn't promise what he'd do if she kept bending over like that.

"Not on my time," he said sharply, "and not in my elevator. Dammit, why argue over something so simple?"

"Go ahead, then. Who am I to argue with the man in charge?"

"'Thank you' might be a more gracious response." Keir squatted down, yanked the shoe free and rose to his feet. "Here. Next time you decide to wear stilts—"

The car shuddered to a halt. Cassie yelped, stumbled, and Keir caught her in his arms.

She caught her breath. So did he. She was pressed tightly against him, her back against his chest, her bottom against his groin. Don't move, he thought, God, don't move…

The doors swooshed open. Keir heard a sound. A snicker? No. A snort of laughter. He swung around, taking Cassie with him, and saw two very interested, all-too-familiar faces.

Cassie gave a little moan of despair. "Your brothers?" she whispered.

Keir nodded.

Sean and Cullen O'Connell simply grinned.

CHAPTER TWO

CASSIE'S day had gone really, really well.

She'd worked a double shift to cover for one of the other girls who'd either come down with the flu or had a new boyfriend—nobody was quite sure which—but that was okay.

No problem. She could use the extra money.

The only thing was that she'd started the first shift tired after a tough, three hour exam, the final one before she got her degree in restaurant management. Cassie had taken the course on the Internet after signing up, mostly out of curiosity, two years ago. The work had been interesting and, to her surprise, she'd done well at it.

Soon, she'd start looking for a job as far from Vegas as she could get. She'd already decided on an employment agency, a place called TopNotch, because the gossip mill said TopNotch provided almost all management employees to the Desert Song.

If it was good enough for the Song, it was good enough for her.

By the time her second shift was drawing to a close, Cassie was totally exhausted. Her mouth felt stiff from constant smiling, her eyes felt tired from the re-circulated air washing over her contacts, and her feet...

No. She wasn't going to think about her feet. Rule One in Cassandra Bercovic's Survival Guide: dancers and waitresses should never think about their feet until they no longer had to stand on them. Once you admitted they hurt, you were in deep trouble.

She was already in trouble.

Cassie winced as she eased one foot just a little way out of its silken, stiletto-heeled prison. Her toes felt as if they'd been jammed into a ball, her arches ached and the soles burned as if a sadist had gone at them with a blowtorch.

She sighed, plucked an empty glass from beside a silent slot machine and put it on her tray.

Toe shoes had been the bane of her existence until she'd given up ballet the day after her seventeenth birthday. Back then, she'd thought bloody feet were only the province of ballerinas.

Talk about being wrong...

Okay. Enough of feeling sorry for herself. Her feet hurt. Big deal. The good news was that she was almost out of here. It had to be close to seven. There was no way to tell because there were never clocks in casinos. The only time that mattered was how long a guest spent at the slots or at the tables.

She knew the time, though. She'd asked Chip on her last stop to put in an order at the bar.

"Pushing 6:15 in the old A.M.," he'd told her.

Thank God.

Cassie swallowed a yawn. One last circuit of the room and that would be it. The casino was almost empty at this hour. Only the diehards played between dawn and breakfast, and there hadn't been too many of them this morning.

"Miss?"

She knew who it was before she looked. The sweaty-faced guy at the dollar slots. Rule Number Two of the Bercovic Survival Guide: you could count on a minimum of one pig turning up, each and every shift.

"Yes, sir?" she said politely.

"Gimme another orange juice. And this time, do like I said, okay? I want a double shot of vodka, not a single."

"It was a double shot the last time, sir," Cassie replied, even more politely.

The man glared as he slapped his empty glass on her tray. She shot a quick look at the tall paper cup that held his coins. Last time she'd come by, it was full. Now, it was almost empty.

"Listen, toots, I can tell the difference between one shot or two, and that wasn't no two. I want a double. You got that?"

Cassie could almost feel her blood pressure soar but she'd been a waitress long enough to manage a smile.

"Yes, sir. I'll be right back with your drink."

Her smile turned into a scowl when she reached the bar.

"Pig," she muttered as she slapped down her tray.

Chip grinned. "Nothing's as much fun as the early morning players, Cass. You should know that by now."

"Yeah, yeah, yeah." Cassie sighed. "Another OJ, double vodka."

"Comin' up." Chip reached for a clean glass. "Guy's an asshole, huh?"

"You got it."

"Well, the shift's almost over."

"How soon?"

Chip pushed back his cuff and checked his watch. "Five minutes to go."

"Hallelujah! I'm so tired I'm liable to fall asleep standing up."

"Yeah. Me, too." He cleared his throat. "Coffee would help, right?"

"I don't know if anything will help. I'm totally wiped."

"Trust me. You need coffee. Espresso, black, lot of sugar to double the jolt."

"You're probably right."

"And some food," Chip said, adding OJ to the vodka. "Which is why I figured we could go someplace for breakfast, say a little place just opened a couple of blocks off the Strip."

Cassie sighed. "Thanks, but all I'm up for is going home, taking a shower and falling into bed."

"Alone," the bartender said, with an easy smile that made it okay, "right?"

Cassie smiled, too. Chip was a nice guy and if she'd been interested in getting involved, he'd have been a good choice—but then, when it came to men and to life, she'd never managed to make good choices. One thing she'd learned, though. When it came to life, you had to take whatever it threw at you.

Men, at least, you could swear off, and she definitely had.

If only she'd remembered that before Keir O'Connell had come on to her at Dawn's wedding.

"Keir keeps looking at you," Dawn had whispered when they had a moment alone after the ceremony.

"Don't be silly," she'd whispered back. "He's probably just trying to remember where he's seen me before."

Dawn had laughed, just as she was supposed to, but it was true, Keir *had* been looking at her, the way a man looks at a woman, giving her those sexy little grins, leaning in closer than necessary to ask if she wanted anything from the buffet, and he'd been so gorgeous in his tux, so dangerous with those dark as midnight eyes...

"If you change your mind about breakfast..." Chip said, and Cassie looked up and smiled.

"Sure."

"Ouch. Was ever a word said with less enthusiasm?"

"Chip, I'm sorry. It's not you, it's me."

"Double ouch. That's the great-granddaddy of all brush-off lines."

Cassie blushed. "Honestly, I'm just—"

"Hey, I'm teasing. It's okay. Can't blame a guy for trying, right?"

"I'm just not dating anybody for a while. You understand?"

"Sure." He put the double OJ and vodka on her tray. "Bet the guy who ordered this hasn't tipped you yet, right?"

"Clever man."

"He gives you any trouble, you need any help, just sing out."

"Will do. Thanks."

"Hey, no need. I live to serve."

Cassie laughed, plucked a couple of cocktail napkins from the stack on the bar and brought the drink to the guy at the dollar slots. She dipped her knees the way you were supposed to, put a napkin beside him and the glass on top of it.

"Your drink, sir."

"I hope you got it right this time."

"Double vodka and orange juice, just as you ordered."

The man picked up the glass, slurped half of it down while he fed tokens into the machine. Cassie started to walk away.

"Hey! You take this back to that bartender and tell him—"

Coins began to cascade from the slot machine. Music played, lights blinked, and the river of silver kept coming.

"Lookit this! I hit the jackpot."

It certainly looked as if he had. Coins were still pouring out.

"You must of brung me luck, little lady." Grinning, the man stuck a beefy paw into the shimmering explosion of silver. "Here. This is for you."

Cassie lifted her eyebrows. "Why, thank—"

The words caught in her throat. He'd handed her two dollars. She narrowed her eyes, opened her mouth—and felt a hand close around her elbow. Inez, her replacement, marched her away from the machine.

"Do not," Inez said through a toothy smile, "tell *el puerco* what you think of him."

"Two bucks," Cassie hissed. "That's what he gave me, after four drinks and a couple of hours worth of nastiness." She craned her head, looked back over her shoulder. "He must have hit for a thousand."

"Six thousand," Inez said, still smiling and still hustling Cassie toward the employees' exit, "and he is the slime of the universe, but you want to keep your job, right?"

"Inez…"

"Remember the rules, Cass. Employees are always polite to guests."

The rules. The Desert Song's rules. Keir O'Connell's rules, not Cassie Bercovic's. If she told the guy what she thought of him, O'Connell would sack her.

Too bad the boss didn't have rules that governed his own behavior.

"Here." Inez took Cassie's tray and handed her the small purse she'd left behind the bar. "Now, go home."

"Once, just once, I'd like to tell a guy like that what I think."

"Wait until you're ready to quit. Then come into the casino and security will give you special dispensation to clobber the sleazebag of the night." Inez grinned. "Okay?"

Cassie sighed. "Okay."

"Until then...you're rude, you're crude, you lose your job."

"I know."

"Good, 'cause the big man's serious when he tells that to employees. If you have a legitimate beef with some SOB, you take it to O'Connell and let him handle it."

Inez was right. That was Keir's policy, and wasn't that amazing because if you wanted to talk about rude, crude sons of bitches, he was your man.

And why did she keep thinking about him this morning? She wasn't going to do it again, except maybe to consider that as bad as the guy up to his wrists in silver was, Keir was worse.

"Okay," Cassie said, with the stretch-the-lips smile she'd learned putting in six nights a week strutting across a stage with the Eiffel Tower on her head. "I'm going home."

"You do that. Just leave Mr. Big Tipper to me." Inez fluttered her lashes. "I'll be so sweet when I talk to him that he'll pass out from a sugar overdose."

Cassie laughed and gave the other woman a quick hug. "Good night."

"You mean, good morning."

"Whatever. Have a good one."

"Yeah. You, too."

Cassie thought about taking the stairs to the basement locker room but she was just too tired and her feet really were killing her. Maybe it was these shoes. They were new, and the straps cut into her flesh.

She pressed the call button for one of the employee elevators. Sighing, she slipped one foot from her shoe and rubbed her cramped toes against the carpet.

Wearing three inch heels wasn't fun, especially if you'd spent most of your life torturing your tootsies.

Rule Number Three of Cassandra Bercovic's Survival Guide, Cassie thought, grimacing as she pressed the call button again. If you started doing *pliés* at seven and high kicks at seventeen, forget about high heels because your feet would be a hundred years older than the rest of you by the time you hit twenty-nine.

The problem was, Rule Number Three was pitched into the dust by Rule Number Four.

The Higher The Heels, The Better The Tips.

It was the truest rule of all, and she needed every penny she could come by if she wanted to hold out for the right management job. She didn't know where she'd find it or when. Her only criteria was that the place had to be small and pretty, and light-years from Las Vegas.

Then she could trade in these torturous stilettos for a nice comfy pair of orthopedics.

The thought made her smile.

Sighing, she slid her shoe back on, stepped out of the other one and flexed her toes.

Except for the one jerk, she'd had a pretty good shift. Two shifts. Most people had been pleasant, the tips had been decent, and the only guy who'd tried to hit on her was so decrepit that she'd almost felt sorry for him.

Cassie glanced up at the unblinking lights on the panel over the cars. What was taking so long? That hot shower and soft bed were calling to her...well, maybe she'd wait on the bed part. She'd sign on to her computer, see if, by some miracle, her grade was waiting in her e-mail in-box. And there was something she wanted to check on, a question she was pretty sure she'd gotten right on the exam but she wanted to look it up and be sure.

Tired or not, she preferred going online early in the day, while things were still relatively quiet in her apartment complex. It had been tough, getting into the habit of hitting the books after you'd been out of school for almost a dozen years, especially when you'd been such a miserable failure while you'd been there the first time.

Maybe that was why she hadn't told anyone she was taking the course. This way, if she flunked out, nobody would know except her. She might have told Dawn, who was her best friend, but she'd sensed that Dawn had enough trouble of her own without having to worry about offering encouragement to a terrified student.

And then Dawn had fallen head over heels in love and she'd plunged into planning a beautiful wedding at Gray's uncle's ranch in Tex—

Cassie stiffened.

Uh uh. She wasn't going there again. Forget Texas. She'd wasted enough time the past month, going over what had happened, what she'd said, what Keir had said, trying to figure out how she'd ended up in that garden, letting him make a fool of her.

Actually, it wasn't was all that difficult to understand. The romantic setting would have softened even the most dedicated cynic. Add buckets of champagne, dreamy music, the no-way-out-of-it amount of time the maid of honor was expected to spend with the best man…

The best man. What a joke. The *worst* man was more like it, and where was that damned elevator?

Cassie banged on the call button.

She missed Dawn. All those late-night chats at the kitchen table, the two of them pigging out on pizza or take-out Chinese. If Dawn were still here, she'd not only have told her about the restaurant management course, she'd

have told her about Keir O'Connell, too, how he'd gone
slumming, how amazed he'd been when she'd stopped him
from making love to her...

...how relieved.

Cassie's mouth thinned.

Oh, his face when she'd told him to stop. All she'd meant
was that things were moving too fast but Keir had blanched
under that all-year tan. He'd let go of her so quickly that
she'd almost fallen.

"Cassie," he'd said, his voice hoarse. "Cassie, I'm so
sorry..."

What he'd meant was, *What the hell was I doing?*

She knew, because she'd seen that look on men's faces
before, when she was a showgirl. You met someone, you
hit it off, things were fine until the guy asked what you did
for a living.

"I dance," she'd say.

"Where?" he'd say.

From there on, it was all downhill.

By the time she'd been desperate enough to strip, she'd
known better than to talk about it.

She wasn't either a showgirl or a stripper anymore but it
didn't matter. She was still Cassie Berk and some things
never changed...and where was that miserable elevator?

To hell with it. History was history. With a little luck
she'd be out of Vegas soon enough. No more hearing the
ping of the slots, even in her sleep. No more guys thinking
she was smiling just for them. No more turning her feet into
aching, leaden weights.

Best of all, no more seeing Keir.

He was away. On vacation, everybody said, as if it were
a miracle the great man would do such a thing.

She'd already known he was going away.

"I'm taking some time off," he'd told her as they sat alone
at one of the little umbrella tables, smiling at each other because
smiling had seemed a good thing to do right then.

He'd said her he was going to New York and then he'd

hesitated as if he were going to tell her something else, and just for a minute, for the tiniest bit of eternity, she'd thought maybe, oh maybe he was going to say, "Cassie, come with me…"

The light panel blinked to life; the elevator doors slid open. Cassie was trying to jam her foot back into her shoe when the doors began to slide shut.

"Hey!"

She lunged forward, hobbled into the car and stepped on some plywood sheets one of the maintenance guys must have left on the floor. One heel sank into the wood.

"Idiot," she mumbled, as the elevator doors closed.

She grimaced, tried to jerk her foot free, but the heel was wedged into a knothole.

"Major idiot," she said, and jerked her foot out of the shoe. Tongue between her teeth, she bent over and began working the shoe free. It wobbled under the pressure of her hand and she knew she'd have to be careful or she'd snap the stupid heel off. It wasn't just high, it was also thin, sharp and unstable.

Too bad she hadn't been wearing this pair of torture devices at Dawn's wedding. If she'd planted a heel like this in Keir's instep, he'd still be limping.

"Dammit," she hissed, "would-you-let-loose?"

The shoe didn't budge. Maybe it had better sense than she did. If *she* hadn't budged, hadn't gone into that garden with him…

How could she have made such an ass of herself? She'd spent her life living by Rule Number Five, or maybe it was Six. Who cared what number it was? The rule was what mattered.

Never Make It With The Boss.

It was the most important rule of all, it let you avoid a whole mess of trouble, and she'd almost broken it. And what about the rules he'd broken? All those sexual harassment things that said employers were not to hit on their employees.

What about that?

She'd been foolish but no question, Keir was to blame for what had happened. Coming on to her, when he was her boss. Maybe he did it all the time. She'd never heard even a hint of gossip but when men who looked like he did—tall, broad-shouldered and altogether gorgeous—they set their own rules.

What was with this damn shoe?

If she never saw Keir again, it would be—

The car jerked to a stop. The doors slid open. She heard someone clear his throat and she almost laughed, thinking what a weird sight she probably made...

"Hello, Cassie."

She froze. That voice. Male. Deep. A little husky. As removed as if they'd never had that midnight encounter in the garden.

But—but it couldn't be. Keir was away. He was—

He was here, looking at her with a smile so polite she wanted to slap it away.

"You," she said, and she knew her loathing for him was in the one word because that polite smile slipped from his face.

"Yeah, that's right. Me." He looked at her foot, then at her face. "Having a problem?" he said, his voice tinged with amusement.

"No," she snapped, "I always stand around like this, with one shoe on and one shoe—"

The car began to move. She hadn't expected it and she jerked back.

"Careful!"

Keir grabbed for her but Cassie flung out a hand and caught the railing.

"Don't touch me!"

"No problem." His voice was cool. "You want to break your neck, be my guest."

"I'm doing just fine on my own."

"Oh, yeah. I can see that." He watched, arms folded, as she tried to pull the shoe free again. "Stop being foolish,

Berk. Let me help—or would you rather I put in a call to Maintenance and have them send up a work crew?''

"What? Those idiots? They're the ones who left this damned piece of wood here in the first place.''

She glared at him, then at her shoe. The truth was, he could probably free it in less time than it would take him to make the call. Besides, if the maintenance guys showed up, they'd have a good laugh and spread the story all over the hotel.

Cassie lifted her chin. "All right.''

"'Thank you' might be a more gracious response.'' Keir squatted down, grabbed the shoe, yanked it free and rose to his feet. "Here. Next time you decide to wear stilts—''

The car jolted to a stop. Cassie stumbled, yelped, and Keir grabbed her before she could fall.

Grabbed her, so that she was pressed back against him, so that she could feel the warmth of his body, feel the swift hardening of it...

Somebody was laughing.

Keir swung around, still holding her. Cassie's eyes widened. Two men were standing at the open doors of the elevator, taking in the scene with big grins on their faces.

They looked nothing like Keir or each other...and looked everything like Keir and each other.

Her heart dropped to her toes.

For days, the staff had been talking about the O'Connell clan, all Mary Elizabeth's daughters and sons, and how they were going to descend on the hotel for the duchess's wedding to Dan Coyle.

"Your brothers?'' Cassie said, even though she already knew the answer.

Keir nodded, his brothers chuckled, and Cassie wondered what the odds were on the bottom falling out of the car so she could simply disappear.

CHAPTER THREE

BEYOND the perimeter of the Desert Song, the Strip was as brightly-lit, as busy and noisy as if it were midday instead of midnight, but everything was hushed deep within the hotel gardens. The lights in the oversized pool had been dimmed and emitted a soft, fairy glow.

Nice, Cullen O'Connell thought, as he drifted on a float in the warm, silky water. You could even see the stars. Not the way they blazed in the blackness over the vast grasslands of the Rift Valley or on a rare, clear night high on the snow-laden slopes of Mount McKinley, but nice, nevertheless.

Even in Vegas, it was nice to know that the stars were still there.

"You counting stars again, like when we were kids?" Sean O'Connell spoke softly, from a float just a few feet away.

"Better to count stars than count cards like you were doing at the blackjack table a little while ago," Cullen said lazily.

Sean chuckled. "Now, Cullen, would I do that? Counting cards is illegal—if you do it when you play a hand, and I was only watching, not playing."

"Counting stars is safer," Cullen said with a smile in his voice.

"Considering that we're back in Sin City, maybe the only thing we should be counting is babes."

"Like that summer, you mean?" Cullen smiled up at the sky. "When I saved my allowance the whole year so I could buy a telescope? And Pop found you using it to girl-watch instead?"

"You mean, Pop found *us* using it."

"Yeah, well, I was easily corrupted."

Sean gave a soft laugh. "I'd almost forgotten that. Remember the blonde in the corner room on the fourteenth floor of the east wing?"

"How could I forget? She was the reason the old man threw out my telescope and paddled my behind so hard I couldn't sit for a week."

"Two days, and admit it, she was worth it."

The men drifted in silence for a while, and then Sean spoke.

"How many times you think we sneaked out here at night, buddy? I figure it must have been at least a couple of hundred."

"Heck, we probably got *caught* a couple of hundred."

"Yeah. And got our bottoms warmed. Never stopped us, though, from sneaking out again."

"That's 'cause it was worth it, coming out here late at night, getting to use the pool without sharing it with a couple of trillion strangers."

The brothers sighed, at ease as they drifted on the water and three decades of shared memories.

"So," Cullen said, "where were you when you found out about Ma's engagement to this guy?"

Sean turned over on the float and cushioned his face on his folded arms.

"Monte Carlo. At a private casino. I was up fifty grand when I got the cable." His voice roughened. "I must have lost ten years of my life, just opening the envelope. I thought—"

"—that Ma had had another heart attack. I know. It was the same for me. I was downloading my e-mail and there was this message marked 'urgent,' with the Desert Song's address on it and I figured…" Cullen sighed. "I was so relieved that it took me a while to start worrying about the actual message, you know? That she's marrying this Dan Coyle, a man nobody knows."

"Keir knows him, and seems to like him."

"True."

"And Ma's crazy about him."

"Well, those are both good signs, right?"

"Right." Sean sighed. "It's good to be back."

"Temporarily."

"Oh, yeah. That goes without saying. I wouldn't want to live in this fishbowl again." Sean dropped his hand and let his fingers glide through the water. "We owe Keir."

"For taking over here, after Pop died? Yeah. Big time."

"He looks… I don't know. Edgy."

"You think?"

"Maybe that's the wrong word. I just get the feeling he's got something on his mind."

"The fox in the elevator, maybe." Cullen grinned. "Man, what a scene to walk in on. Keir, holding an armful of female, looking at us as if he wished he could have dropped right through the floor of that car…"

Sean rolled off his float and into the water. "You think there was something really going on there?"

"In an elevator, in the Desert Song? That's not big brother's style. He's too buttoned up to try something like that."

"Too bad we didn't get much chance to torment him about it."

"Yeah. Bree's and Meg's timing sort of screwed things up." Sean's voice warmed as he spoke his sisters' names. "It's good to see the two of them. Last time we were all together was, what, Christmas?"

"I know. Well, it's tough, with you traipsing around the world, me in New York, Bree in San Francisco, Meg in Boston, Fallon God knows where—"

"Paris, last I heard, for what she calls a fashion shoot."

"Meanwhile, Keir's trapped here in Vegas."

"You think that's the way he feels?"

"It's the way I'd feel, in his place."

Cullen hoisted himself out of the pool and dragged the float up beside him.

"You know what? I'm going to get him alone and ask him. I mean, maybe he wants to go on managing the Song, but if he doesn't... Ma's okay now. She looks wonderful, in fact. Seems to me it's time we made other arrangements, like convincing her to hire someone to take over."

"Someone *is* going to take over," Keir said, stepping out of the shadows. "Under the duchess's supervision, of course."

"Of course," Sean said, smiling. "How'd you get her to agree to that?"

"Actually, she suggested it." Keir loosened his tie and tucked his hands into his pockets. "Her doctors gave her a clean bill of health and she's been chomping at the bit, wanting to get back to work."

"She's up to handling things alone? Well, with the help of a Chief of Ops?"

"She won't have to. She's going to be a married lady this time tomorrow, remember?"

"Actually, we wanted to talk to you about that. This guy Coyle. He's okay?"

"Yes. Definitely okay."

"He'd better be."

"I think he was pretty okay to you guys when you tried that CIA interrogation at dinner." Keir grinned. "Considering he's a retired captain of detectives with the New York City P.D., he let you get off easy."

"Hey," Sean said, straight-faced, "you can never be too careful about a man you're going to call 'Daddy.'"

"Tell him that, why don't you?" Keir said, his tongue firmly tucked in his cheek.

"I did. That's when I decided he was probably all right."

"Because?"

"Because he said he'd slug me one, if I ever tried it."

The three brothers laughed. Then Sean climbed out of

the pool, dumped his float over a *chaise longue* and thumbed his wet hair out of his eyes.

"So, let me get this straight. Ma's going to hire somebody to manage the place, and he'll report to her and Dan?"

"That's the plan. Just to set your minds at ease, I trust Dan completely, not only because I ran an in-depth check on him before I brought him into the Song a few years back but also because I've gotten to know him well. He's definitely one of the good guys. And he knows the Song, inside and out." Keir shoved aside the damp towel Sean had tossed over a lounge chair and sat down. "That sound okay to you two?"

"It sounds fine," Sean said.

"Fine," Cullen echoed. "But where does that leave you?"

Keir cleared his throat. "I'm, uh, I'm moving on."

The simple words stopped conversation. Until now, Keir hadn't realized how ominous they sounded.

"Moving on?" Sean said. "Where?"

Keir hesitated. His mother had looked at him as if he'd lost his sanity when he'd told her his plans. Would his brothers?

"I'm going east. I bought a business in Connecticut."

"You serious?"

"Dead serious. It looks like it's going to be a lot of work. I mean, it's small, but I think, given time, I can build it into something."

"What kind of business?"

Keir shrugged. "A small one, like I said."

"He's being deliberately vague," Sean said to Cullen, as if Keri weren't there.

"Yup. In fact, I get the feeling BB doesn't want to tell us what this business is," Cullen replied, his grin hidden by the darkness.

"Don't call me that!"

"Can you imagine? He doesn't want to call him BB and he doesn't want to tell us what this business is." Sean gave a deep sigh. "What's the good of having a brother if he won't let you in on his secrets?"

"A Big Brother," Cullen said solemnly.

"Uh huh." There was a pause. "With a pair of capital B's, for short."

"Will you stop calling me that? And I didn't say it was a secret!"

"Should we tell him he didn't have to?" said Cullen. "Should we remind him that we're his very own flesh and blood and we can read him like a book?"

Keir looked from Cullen to Sean. Despite all their teasing, they were worried about him. He knew, because he'd overheard more of their conversation than he'd let on. Well, why not tell them now? Get it over with, instead of dragging it out until after the wedding tomorrow. That was what he'd planned but being pronounced insane by all five of his siblings at once might be just a little intimidating.

"Okay." He took a deep breath. "You want to know what kind of business I bought?" Another deep breath. "A vineyard."

For what seemed an eternity, neither Sean nor Cullen said anything. Sean was the first to break the silence.

"Did you say, vineyard? As in, where they grow grapes and make wine?"

"That's right. With a small restaurant as part of the set-up."

"A vineyard," Sean repeated.

"Yes."

"In Connecticut," Cullen added. "With a small restaurant as—"

"Dammit, will you stop that? Yes. A vineyard. And a restaurant. And I don't care if you guys think I'm nuts or what, I'm glad I bought— Hey! Hey, what're you doing?"

What they were doing was clapping him on the back hard enough to have sent a smaller man to his knees.

"Man, that's terrific," Cullen said happily. "I mean, it's

crazy as hell but it's time you did something crazy. Right, Sean?"

"Absolutely. It's so off the wall, it sounds like something I could have done."

"And that's a compliment?" Keir said, laughing.

"Damn right. Listen, you need to get in touch with anybody who's into wine, let me know. I took a marker I never got around to collecting from a guy playing *chemin de fer* last summer. His family owns a vineyard in Burgundy."

"And if you need legal advice, I'm your man," Cullen said. "I know you have your own attorney but since you'll be doing the deal closer to my turf, back east—"

"Wait a minute." Keir stepped back and looked from one of his brothers to the other. "So, you don't think I'm ready for a rubber room?"

"Well, of course we do but then, we've always thought that. Right, Cullen?"

"Absolutely right." Cullen gave Keir a light punch in the shoulder. "Seriously, congratulations."

"Yeah. I mean, thanks."

"Just for the record, I'm impressed."

A smile curved Keir's mouth. "Yeah?"

"Yeah. Sounds like an interesting proposition."

"Well, that's good to hear because the vote, so far, is three to one that I've lost all my marbles."

"Who's voting?"

"The duchess. My accountant. And my lawyer pretty much made it unanimous."

"Ma'll come around. As for the accountant and the lawyer—all the more reason to dump them."

"You think?"

"Absolutely. Megan'll be your CPA. I'll be your attorney. We'll only be a couple of hours away and besides, why deal with people who'll look for the hole in your head each time you sit down at the table?"

Keir laughed. "You have a way with words, pal, you

know that?'' His smile tilted. ''You want to know the truth, there've been moments I've doubted my own sanity.''

''Just because you're starting to live dangerously? Hey, that's what life's all about.'' Sean elbowed Cullen. ''You got all this straight? The man's bought himself a vineyard. He bought himself a restaurant. And if it hadn't been for us, he'd have made it in the elevator with Cinderella.''

Keir's mouth tightened. He'd been expecting this ever since his brothers walked in on the scene with Cassie.

Then why did the teasing words make his belly knot?

''We were not about to make it in the elevator, as you so delicately put it.''

''Whatever you say, big brother.''

''I hardly know the lady.''

''Well, that's good news for me. Just tell me her name, give me her number—''

''Keep away from her.''

Keir's voice was suddenly tense with warning. Cullen and Sean stared at him. He glared back, and then he groaned.

Cullen was only kidding but even if he wasn't, so what? If he wanted to hit on Cassie, let him.

''I mean,'' he said carefully, ''we embarrassed her enough. Besides, she's an employee. She works in the hotel. She's a cocktail waitress.''

''Well, that certainly explains why the two of you were wrapped around each other. Doesn't it, Sean?''

Keir folded his arms. ''You're never going to leave me alone about this, are you?''

''No,'' Sean agreed pleasantly, ''we're not.''

''Look, the elevator stopped and Cassie was in it. And—''

''And?'' Cullen said, with a lift of his eyebrows.

''And,'' Keir said briskly, ''her heel was stuck.'' Two pairs of eyebrows lifted. He decided to ignore the warning signs. ''Somebody from Maintenance had left some plywood on the floor, and her heel got wedged in a knothole.''

Sean gave a deep sigh. "Dangerous combination, ply-wood and elevators."

Despite himself, Keir's mouth twitched. "Listen, I'm warning you both—"

"No, it's cool," said Cullen. "We understand. As some men get older, they need more of, uh, more of a stimulus before they can get it on."

"Older? I'm one year older. One year!"

"He's right," Sean said. "It wasn't senile male hormones, it was a galloping case of ZTS."

"Okay. It's not going to work. I've explained what happened. You want to get some more mileage out of it, go on. Be my guest."

"Trust us," Sean replied solemnly, "we will."

Keir looked from one of his brothers to the other and saw the laughter dancing in their eyes. A familiar warmth spread through his veins. This was the way it had always been, two of them needling the other, and it had never mattered which two it was because it changed from day to day. Hell, it changed from minute to minute.

But what bonded them together would never change. Shared memories and shared blood would always unite and sustain them, just as it had when they were growing up. Being the sons of Ruarch O'Connell had not been easy, despite the duchess's misty-eyed memories.

He felt a catch in his throat. He'd missed his brothers. Missed this. The teasing, the laughter, the knowledge that nobody in the world knew him the way they did.

"All right." He nodded, sighed, offered all the signs of peaceful surrender. "You guys want details, you'll get them. Just come in a little closer..."

He moved fast, as if they were all still kids and these were the old times, when they'd played their own version of touch football whenever they'd been in one place long enough to find a flat field. He took Sean out first, his shoulder connecting with Sean's flat belly and then he spun and got Cullen before he could sidestep. Both of them yelped and fell backward into the pool hard enough to raise a geyser of water that rivaled Old Faithful.

A spill of feminine laughter erupted behind Keir. He swung around and saw his three sisters standing next to one of the softly-lighted palm trees that ringed the pool.

"Hey." He grinned. Briana, Fallon and Megan grinned back.

"And to think," Fallon said archly, "that Mom sent us to find you gentlemen because she was afraid you were sitting around, having a long, solemn talk about what would happen now that BB's leaving."

Keir raised one dark eyebrow. "You see those guys in the pool? One of the things that put 'em there was calling me Big Brother."

Megan rose on her toes and peered past Keir. "Poor babies," she crooned.

Something in Briana's smile made the hair rise on the back of Keir's neck.

"What?"

Bree fluttered her lashes. "Enjoy your swim," she purred.

He yelped as his brother's hands clamped around his ankles. Keir hit the water hard, went under and came up, sputtering and laughing, between Sean and Cullen.

"Is this the respect you show your big brother?"

Cullen sighed. "All of a sudden, he wants the title back."

"Damn right." Keir smiled. "You know what? It's great to have you home."

"We agree," Sean said, and he and Cullen proved it by shoving Keir right back under the water.

Keir awoke at five minutes before six the next morning. He reached out and shut off his alarm clock before its shrill cry could pierce his foggy brain, then sat up and swung his feet to the floor.

Four hours sleep was all he'd had. He and his brothers and sisters had ended up here in his suite, where they'd sat talking and laughing for hours. There'd been a lot of catching up to do. Only the prospect of having to look bright-eyed for their mother's wedding had finally sent them scattering at almost two in the morning.

Keir yawned, got to his feet and walked into the bathroom. The wedding wasn't until noon but he needed time to check on things, make sure the flowers, the music, the food and champagne were as close to perfect as he could get them.

It wasn't every day a man had the chance to oversee his mother's wedding, he thought as he stepped into the shower.

He had some last minute things to do for himself, too. Falling asleep last night, he'd decided there was no sense in delaying his departure. The sooner he left Vegas and began his new life in Connecticut, the better.

This morning he'd phone his attorney, tell him to fax some documents to Cullen's New York office, then instruct his accountant to fax his files to Megan's office in Boston. He'd already arranged for Deer Run's vintner to stay on, but the woman who managed the restaurant had accepted a job in Florida.

"Too many cold New England winters for me," she'd said.

That meant he'd need a new manager.

The restaurant was handsome and the food was great. Service had been a little erratic—his main course came out at the same time as his soup—but all that could be dealt with. Instinct told him there were probably other details that needed improving.

He didn't know what, specifically. Restaurants weren't his specialty. For the last six years his talent had been managing people and if he'd learned one thing, it was that the key to success was finding the right people, then trusting them enough to do the job.

Finding the right people was relatively simple. Whenever he'd needed a manager, someone with the necessary combination of talent and brass, he'd turned to the TopNotch Employment Agency.

They'd never let him down yet.

Well, why not continue dealing with TopNotch? They had contacts everywhere; they'd sent him people from virtually every state in the union.

Keir stepped from the shower and wrapped a towel around his hips.

Okay. He'd phone TopNotch, lay out what he wanted in a manager for the restaurant and leave finding the right person in their more than capable hands. Then he could devote himself to this new challenge. Deer Run. Wine-making. Life in the quiet hills of Connecticut, instead of the fast neon lanes of Vegas.

Maybe he'd even find himself a woman. Someone special. There hadn't been anyone special, not for a very long time.

Swift as a heartbeat, an image flickered in his mind. He saw a woman in a long, old-fashioned gown that clung to her lush curves with each whisper of the wind…

"Hell," he said, and blanked his thoughts to everything but his mother's wedding.

Promptly at noon, he stood with his brothers and sisters at one side of the altar. Mary had insisted that all her daughters and sons give her away. Dan's grown children stood near their father. Everyone was smiling.

Smiling—and quietly weeping.

Keir could hear his sisters sniffling into their lace hankies. He glanced at his brothers. Their eyes glittered in a way that told him their throats were as tight with emotion as his.

"…pronounce you man and wife," the justice of the peace said.

Dan took Mary in his arms. Keir hugged his brothers, kissed his sisters…and suddenly found himself scanning the room filled with family and friends for a glimpse of a woman with sea-green eyes and coal-black hair.

She wasn't there. Why would she be? And why should he be looking for her? There wasn't a reason in the world to see her ever again.

"Keir," his mother said.

He turned and took the duchess in his arms.

"I'm happy for you, Ma." Dan held out his hand and Keir shook it. "I'm happy for you both."

Mary laid her hand against his cheek. "You're leaving soon, aren't you?"

Keir drew a breath. "Yes. Tomorrow." He smiled at Dan. "Now that I know you're safe in good hands, and happy."

"I want you to be happy, too, Keir," Mary said softly.

"I already am."

His mother's eyes filled. "You need something more."

Hours later as he packed, Keir thought about what his mother had said, and wondered if she was right.

CHAPTER FOUR

Bradley Airport, Connecticut, six weeks later:

CASSIE'S plane touched down on the runway just as the first bolt of lightning tore the sky apart.

"Glad that didn't happen when we were still up there," the woman sitting next to her said.

Cassie agreed. She was nervous enough, considering that she'd flown east to take a job, sight unseen.

She took down her carry-on bag and joined the line exiting the plane.

An incredible job, from the sound of it. It was, just as the headhunter at TopNotch had said, an excellent opportunity. A management position at a small but elegant restaurant. An apartment, free of cost, fully furnished and right on the premises. And, best of all, a salary she'd figured had to be a typo until she'd cleared her throat and asked.

How could she have said no?

"Your references have checked out, Ms. Berk," the headhunter had assured her. "The manager of Tender Grapes seems quite pleased with your qualifications and since the owner's left hiring a replacement in her hands, the job is yours if you want it."

"Just like that? She doesn't want to meet me or anything?"

The headhunter had smiled an unctuous smile that Cassie suspected was meant to be reassuring, but which had exactly the opposite effect.

"Just like that, Miss Berk. The lady trusts my judgment."

Cassie was nobody's fool. Something about the whole

setup was off. Sure, she had her degree in restaurant management and several years experience working as a waitress under her belt, plus all the time she'd put in working in bars and lounges, even if some of it hadn't exactly involved waiting tables or working the cash register, but surely there had to be more qualified people.

What was the catch? Had the place been condemned by the Board of Health? Had the chef tried to poison the diners? Was the owner demented? Better still, why was the current manager so desperate to hire a replacement?

"She's not," the headhunter had assured her a little too quickly. "She's eager, that's all. She'd like to hire someone, spend a couple of days training her, then move on."

Cassie figured the truth was more complicated than that but beggars couldn't be choosers. The job was too good to pass up. So was the chance to get out of Vegas.

Ever since what she thought of as the elevator incident, she'd had waited for somebody to point a finger at her, shriek "Elevator!" and burst out laughing.

She knew that was silly. Keir certainly wouldn't have told anybody he'd been party to such a farce. Neither would his brothers and anyway, all three of the O'Connells had left the day after the wedding.

Good riddance. If there was any decency in life, she'd never see Keir again.

Cassie hurried to the baggage area and waited for her luggage.

The deciding factor in her decision had been a practical one. The restaurant was paying her airfare and moving expenses. A couple of thousand dollars saved was a couple of thousand dollars toward the future. Why waste it?

The luggage belt lurched to life. Cassie stepped forward as suitcases began their circuit of the baggage pickup area. Her suitcase would be easy to spot, thanks to the bright red bow on the handle that she'd taken from one of the pizza boxes at the party last night.

The girls she worked with had given her a fine send-off. Pizza, wine, even a cake.

Good Luck, Cassie, the icing on it had said. Everyone had hugged her and kissed her and laughed, and she'd joined in because that was better than bursting into tears and admitting that this all might all be a mistake.

Her suitcase finally appeared, big red bow and all. Cassie leaned in and hoisted it off the belt.

"You're so brave," Inez had said, "to move to a place you don't know and take on such a big job."

Bravery, she thought as she lugged her suitcase toward the car rental counter, had nothing to do with it. In fact, she was scared spitless. Not that she'd ever admit it to anyone. If life had taught her one great lesson, it was that the best way—the only way—to deal with fear was to look it in the eye and laugh.

The line at the counter was mercifully short. Cassie put down her suitcase.

Besides, being scared—okay, terrified—didn't change the truth. She wanted this fresh start more than she'd ever wanted anything in years. Hadn't she been working toward this moment? Managing a small, established restaurant for a salary that still made her blink was what all the studying was about. And if the new job sounded as if might come with problems attached...

Why think that way? Maybe she was wrong. Maybe her résumé sounded brilliant instead of pathetic. Besides, it was time for a change. A big one. You couldn't go on working in a place when you disliked the job, the customers, the people who owned it...

Not true. She didn't dislike Mary O'Connell. It was Keir she disliked. Disliked? Cassie snorted, loud enough so the guy ahead of her looked around, his expression noncommittal, though it changed fast enough when he saw her.

"Hello," he said, and smiled with all his teeth.

"Goodbye," she said, and didn't bother with the smile.

The guy turned the color of a rutabaga and she knew she'd been curt to the point of rudeness, but so what?

If you're rude or crude, you're out of here.

That had been Keir's dictum. He'd put it differently, couched it in some smooth talk about the importance of treating guests with respect at all times, but the employees had boiled it down to one simple phrase.

She could be as rude and crude as she liked. O'Connell had nothing to do with her life anymore. Besides, the guy who'd just come on to her was big and good-looking. Men like that deserved to be put in their places.

The line shuffled forward.

Too bad she hadn't put Keir in his instead of fleeing right after those elevator doors opened. She knew how it must have looked to his brothers. Imagine if they'd seen what had happened in the garden, when she'd been in Keir's arms not by accident but because she'd wanted to be, wanted his mouth on hers, wanted to feel all that heat and hunger...

The woman behind her cleared her throat. Cassie blinked. The line had moved forward while she'd been wasting time thinking about a man who hadn't wanted her for anything but a roll in the hay—and had ended up having second thoughts about that.

He was ancient history, not worth a minute of her time. She hadn't even joined in the gossip about where he'd gone, or why, after the duchess's wedding.

Some of the girls she'd worked with said there'd been no room for him at the Song anymore, but she didn't buy that. Maybe maternal love was blind, but all you had to do was see Mary Elizabeth and Keir together to know how much the duchess loved him.

As for where he'd gone... New York, someone said. Or Paris, something about a big French hotel corporation hiring him. Either place could have him. She'd had a schoolgirl crush that got out of hand. That was the only reason she'd ended up making an ass of herself that night, Cassie thought coolly, and stepped up to the counter.

*   *   *

Moments later, she was behind the wheel of a rental car and on the highway, feeling better and better as the tires ate up the miles. The road was wide, the traffic light, and the storm had moved off. Trees flashed by on either side, dressed in the brilliant orange, red and gold of a New England fall. When she let down the window, sweet, rain-fresh air filled the car.

Cassie took a deep breath. Nice. Very nice, especially for someone who'd never been further east than Austin.

This was going to be great. A good decision, a good move... A good career step.

Eyes glued to the road, she dug her hand into her purse and pulled out the written directions the headhunter had given her. The only part that looked sticky came after she left the highway and took a state road that intersected the town road that led to the turnoff for Tender Grapes.

"Louise Davenport—the manager you'll be replacing— says to keep your eyes peeled," the headhunter had said. "The turnoff from Fenton Road to the restaurant comes up quickly and it isn't well-marked."

"But there *is* a sign, right?"

"Oh, yes. Ms. Davenport says it's just not as visible as it might be. She says it makes people turn up late for their dinner reservations all the time."

Why not change the sign? Cassie had thought, but she hadn't been foolish enough to say it.

"No problem," she'd told the headhunter, in her most businesslike manner.

Once you'd made a blind leap into a new life, why worry about a sign?

Almost two hours later, Cassie knew she'd been wrong. She should have worried about the sign. "Hard to see" was one thing, but this sign was invisible even after two U-turns and three increasingly slow crawls up and down Fenton Road in search of it.

And, just to jazz things up, the storm that had greeted her at the airport seemed to be returning with a vengeance.

The sky was darkening; thunder, accompanied by occasional jagged spears of lightning, rumbled overhead.

Where was that damned sign?

Cassie pulled onto the shoulder of the road. She was already fifteen minutes late. Well, it was the Davenport woman's fault, for giving her such lousy directions. Exasperated, she plucked them from the passenger seat and read them again.

Highway 84 to Route 44. Yes. Proceed east for twelve miles. Yes. Make a right onto Fenton Road, which was at the intersection with the gas station on the left, the hardware store on the right. Yes.

Yes?

This *was* Fenton Road, wasn't it? That place where she'd made the turn, where she'd spotted the store with the lawn mowers and a bunch of other strange-looking machines out front *was* a hardware store…wasn't it?

Cassie sighed, dropped the directions in her lap and drove back the way she'd come. Rain pattered against the windshield, lightly at first, then more heavily. The intersection was just ahead. Gas station, check. Hardware store, che…

"Oh, hell," she said wearily.

It wasn't a hardware store, it was a place that sold lawn and yard equipment. Well, how would you know that, unless you were a local?

Fifteen more minutes wasted, finding the correct intersection, then making the turn onto Fenton Road. The rain had turned into a downpour so hard that she kept waiting for Noah to sail past in his ark, except old Noah couldn't have navigated an ark or even a rowboat on a road like this. It was too narrow, too twisty, too overhung with tall trees that muscled right up to the blacktop.

This had to be the right road, but where was the sign? Not that it mattered. She was so late now that she could kiss the new job goodbye. Cassie had no difficulty imagining Louise Davenport giving her a cold eye and saying sorry, she'd changed her mind, she wasn't about to hire someone who turned up an hour late, even if Tender Grapes was desperate because, face it, a place had to be desperate to—

Was that a sign?

Cassie stood on the brakes. Not too bright on a wet, leaf-strewn road. The car shuddered and stopped. She backed up cautiously. Yes. It was a sign, a small one, half-buried in a tangle of wet leaves and shrubs, with what looked to be a wagon track leading into the woods just beyond it.

She craned her neck, narrowed her eyes, did everything humanly possible to read what the sign said. She couldn't, not from the dry warmth of the car.

Cassie sighed, listened to the rain drumming on the roof, then watched the water overwhelming the windshield wipers. She looked down at her plum-colored silk suit, her black suede pumps...

A long, weary breath and she stepped out into the deluge. It took less than a second.

Goodbye, frighteningly expensive, viciously conservative hairdo. Goodbye, equally expensive, equally conservative suit. Goodbye, pumps with the stylish-yet-comfortable-lady executive heels, which sank into the muck with each step as she plodded to the sign and scraped away wet debris and leaves.

Goodbye, perfect-yet-conservative hundred-dollar manicure, she thought, and almost wept.

Yes, this was the sign. *Deer Run Vineyard,* it said. *Tender Grapes Restaurant, Luncheon and Dinner Tuesday thru Thursday, by Reservation Only.*

Deer Run Vineyard?

Cassie shoved her dripping wet hair out of her eyes, thought about wringing out the hem of her skirt, thought about pointing the car back toward the airport and flying home so she could wring the neck of the headhunter who'd sent her on this debacle of a trip...

Except, Las Vegas wasn't home. Not anymore. She *had* no home. No apartment. No job. Nothing to go back to.

No one to go back to.

She was completely alone.

The realization, which she'd so carefully managed to hold in abeyance until now, drove the breath from her lungs. She got into the car oblivious to the wet, to the cold seeping into her bones, folded her hands in her lap and stared blindly at the rain.

Alone.

But she'd been alone before.

Cassie closed her eyes. The truth was, she'd always been alone, even when she was a little girl. A mother who drank, the faintest ghost-memory of a father...

Her eyes flew open. What was this foolishness? When had she ever wallowed in self-pity?

"Never," she said firmly, and turned the key in the ignition.

She'd been a hell of a lot more alone when she was seventeen than she was now. She'd dropped out of high school with only six months to go before graduation, packed her things and left.

Cassie lifted her chin, put the car in Drive and turned onto the wagon track that led into the forest.

Just left, when she was almost seventeen, without an idea of what she was going to do, where she wanted to go, how she'd support herself. She'd taken her baby-sitting money, all one hundred and fifty bucks of it, shoved the least threadbare of her clothes into a backpack, walked the five miles to the bus station and bought a ticket for the first bus out of Denver.

That, she thought firmly, as low branches reached for the car like hungry fingers, *that* was being alone.

And she'd survived.

Maybe there were things she didn't want to remember, things that had made surviving possible, but she was older now, and wiser.

She had skills, too. She was a dancer, could still be one despite her bad knee, if this job didn't work out. All those years learning tap and ballet, at first because it had been better going to the neighborhood after-school program than going home and then because she'd come to love the hard work and discipline of dance. And, after that, the better part of a decade doing high kicks and struts...

She couldn't do the high kicks anymore but she could still dance for her supper if she had to, the same as she could serve a roomful of hungry customers, courteously and efficiently.

The one thing she'd never do again was strip, not if it meant taking a job cleaning toilets instead.

And she'd never wait tables in a place where the customers were jerks, like that guy in the casino the day she'd seen Keir for the last time, when he'd put his arms around her in that elevator and even though she'd known he was just trying to keep her from falling, she'd felt...she'd felt...

Cassie grimaced. "Oh, for God's sake," she said with disgust.

She was older and wiser, and done with men. Besides, why was she thinking in terms of defeat?

Through the thinning trees ahead, she could see a clearing and a handsome red barn with gently rolling hills behind it. The rain made it difficult to see much more, but she could make out a tall structure—a turret, maybe—and the rooflines of a house on the ridge of one of the hills.

This had to be her destination.

Her heart thumped.

Yes. It was. This sign was bigger and easy to read.

Welcome to Deer Run. And, in smaller letters, *Tender Grapes Restaurant.*

Except for a black SUV and a couple of nondescript cars, the parking lot was almost empty. Cassie pulled into a space, shut off the engine and tried to gather herself together. Okay. The good news was that she'd finally found the place. The bad news was that she was close to an hour late.

She pulled down the sun visor, looked into the mirror

behind it, and groaned. Who'd want to employ the creature staring back at her? She looked as if she'd been dragged through the mud.

Cassie popped open her purse, took out a comb and tugged it through her wet hair. Great. Now she looked as if somebody had plastered a black wig to her head. And what was that? Mascara, dammit! Quickly, she wet the tip of a finger and rubbed at her eye. As if a smudge of mascara was going to make the difference between looking like something that just crept out of the primordial ooze and a competent, businesslike manager.

She snapped her purse shut.

Never mind what she looked like, or that Louise Davenport would either faint or shriek with laughter at the sight of her. Never mind that she'd probably blown this job offer. She'd come a very long distance and she wasn't about to bolt and run now.

She had never run, not from anything, unless you counted that night in Texas and that had been a different situation, entirely.

Mouth set in a grim line, she stepped from the car, marched across the gravel to the red barn and the door marked *WELCOME*. The rain picked that moment to stop, just as if somebody had turned off a faucet, and a watery sun peeked out from behind a cloud.

Too bad she wasn't into omens. On the other hand, maybe Louise Davenport was. It was a thought worth keeping.

Did she knock? Or did that "welcome" sign really mean "enter"? Cassie took a breath, put her hand on the doorknob...

The door swung open. A tall woman with iron-gray hair stared at her, then reached for her hand.

"There you are. I'd about given up." The woman cocked her head. "You are Cassie Berk, aren't you?"

"Yes. Yes, I am. And I'm awfully sorry I'm so late, and that I'm such a mess, but—"

"Nonsense." The woman drew Cassie forward into what was obviously a small, handsomely furnished reception area. "You're here, and just in time. Oh, have I introduced myself? I'm Louise. Louise Davenport."

"Yes. I mean, how do you do, Miss—"

"Miss Berk, I'd love to chat but as it is, I'm going to just about make my flight."

Cassie blinked. "Your flight?"

"Umm. I'd hoped to show you around a bit but I'm afraid I can't take the time."

"Oh, but—but Miss Davenport…"

"Louise," the other woman said, as she collected a raincoat, purse and umbrella from a chair.

"Louise. I don't understand. Don't you at least want to ask me some questions?"

Louise looked puzzled. "I already hired you. Why would I ask you anything?"

"Well—well, we've never met. There must be some things you want to talk about."

"Very well. I suppose there are."

Cassie let out a breath. "Good. Because I have some things I want to ask—"

"Are you good at getting along with people?"

"I'm fine at getting along with people."

"Even chefs?" Louise laughed gaily. "Chefs with big egos, touchy temperaments and shiny knives?"

Cassie stared at the woman. "That's a joke, right?"

"Certainly. Oh, of course it's a joke, my dear. What else would it be?"

The truth? Cassie took a quick step back. All at once, returning to Las Vegas, job or no job, apartment or no apartment, seemed like an eminently viable option.

"Miss Davenport. Um. Louise. I'm starting to think there's been a mistake."

"Oh, no mistake, I assure you." Louise slid on her raincoat and buttoned it. "I must tell you, though, I think you're a brave woman, taking on this place." Her eyes darkened. "And that man."

"What man?"

"The headhunter told me she explained everything to you, the reason for the generous salary and the rental-free apartment. My hands are clean. I didn't hide a thing, not a thing, I mean, what's the sense? So many applicants, so many people who've come and gone in two or three day's time... Well." Smiling she held out her hand. "Good luck, Cassie."

"No." Cassie backed away from the outstretched hand. "I mean, you can't just leave. You have to show me the ropes and—and besides, I'm not sure I want to—"

"Louise!"

Both women jumped. The roar came from the top of a narrow staircase on the other side of the room. The voice was male and human, but it made Cassie think of an enraged lion.

"Louise, is the woman here yet?"

Louise made a face. "His bite is every bit as bad as his bark," she hissed, and took a breath. "Yes," she said loudly, "she got here a couple of minutes ago."

"Well, let's hope she's not as addle-brained as the last one you interviewed."

That voice! Oh God, that voice. Cassie became very still.

Louise squared her shoulders as she turned toward the stairs.

"Whatever she is," she said coolly, "she'll have to do, because I am leaving."

"Louise." The voice oozed charm as footsteps started down the steps. "What can I do to make you stay? I've already offered to double your salary. Can't you—"

"No," Louise said firmly, "I can't."

She slipped past Cassie, walked into the rain and slammed the door behind her.

I should be right on her heels, Cassie thought wildly, as

the booted feet and worn jeans of the man came into view. It couldn't be. It couldn't...

"I don't believe it," Keir said on a shocked whisper. He widened his eyes, shook his head a little as he stared across the room, and Cassie knew exactly how he felt, as if he were having a hideous nightmare and couldn't wake up.

"I don't, either," she said, and she turned away from that face she'd never intended to see again and reached for the door.

CHAPTER FIVE

CASSIE? Cassie, here at Deer Run?

No. Absolutely not. Keir had never been prone to hallucinations but he figured he must be having one now.

Dreaming about Cassie—hot, middle-of-the-night dreams that he thought he'd left behind way back in adolescence—was one thing. Conjuring up an illusion was another, except an illusion wouldn't drip water onto the floor, or look at him as if he was something out of her worst nightmare.

The door banging shut behind her, hard enough to rattle a display of corkscrews, brought him back to reality.

Illusions didn't slam doors.

Keir gave himself a mental shake and went after her. He heard an engine roar to life as he ran down the last steps and out the door, but the car hurtling down the driveway belonged to Louise.

Cassie was just slipping behind the wheel of hers.

"Cassie!"

She didn't even turn her head. Keir snarled an oath, reached through the open window and grabbed her hand just as she was jamming the key into the ignition. He yanked the door open.

"Get out of that car!"

"Keep away from me, O'Connell!"

"I'll say it one more time, lady. Get out of the car."

"Who in hell do you think you are?"

"Are you getting out," he said, curling his hand around her wrist, "or am I going to drag you out?"

"Let me point something out to you, mister. This is not the Desert Song Hotel. I don't work for you anymore. I don't have to click my heels and obey your orders or—"

"Okay. Okay, Berk, that's it."

Cassie yelped as he flung the door open, reached inside and lifted her out from behind the wheel. She fought back, gripping the steering wheel, then the door handle, kicking and cursing and pounding his shoulders, but he was bigger, stronger and determined.

No way was she leaving yet. He had questions. What in hell was she doing here? And why was he torn between the desire to send her packing and the hope that maybe she'd come all this distance because she'd been having the same dreams that had been plaguing him?

"Okay," he said roughly, "what's it going to be? Do I get some answers now, or do I have to carry you inside and tie you to a chair until I get them?"

As if she had a choice, Cassie thought furiously. His threat was all too real. Hadn't he just dragged her out of the car?

"Put me down," she said through her teeth.

"Answer the question first. Are you going to stay put?"

"Am I supposed to be afraid of you? Because I'm not."

"Is that a yes?"

"Put—me—down!"

He did, lowering her slowly to her feet, his eyes flat and dark. She wrenched her arm free, took a step back and met his cold look with one of her own.

"Just for the record, if you try and manhandle me again, you'll regret it."

"Why'd you run?"

"A lesson I learned, living in the desert. You see a snake, you get out of its way as fast as you can."

Keir folded his arms over his chest. "Very amusing. Now, explain yourself."

"I beg your pardon?"

"I want to know what you're doing here."

"Exactly my question, O'Connell. What are *you* doing here?"

Unconsciously, Cassie copied his action, which forced her wet silk sweater and jacket to press icily against her skin. Great. Just great. She was a billion miles from home, cold, wet and angry as hell because despite what she'd just told him, she'd already figured out what Keir was doing here. She just couldn't bring herself to believe it.

"At Deer Run?"

"No," she snapped, "at a watering hole in the middle of the Kalahari. Yes, of course, at Deer Run."

His eyes narrowed. "I own it."

Oh, hell. "You own it."

"That's what I said."

"The restaurant, too?"

He nodded. "That's right."

The confirmation was just what she'd expected. Still, it hit her with the force of a blow. She'd wanted to believe this was just some awful coincidence and there'd be a simple explanation for his presence.

Well, there *was* a simple explanation. He owned the place.

Goodbye new job, new career, new start.

"Your turn, Berk. What are *you* doing here?"

Cassie lifted her chin. "The agency sent me."

"What agency?"

"The employment agency."

"The employment agency?"

"If you repeat everything I say, this is going to be an awfully stupid conversation. You asked TopNotch to hire a manager for your restaurant."

"So?" The anger in his eyes gave way to confusion. "What's that have to do with…"

She knew the instant he figured it out. His dark eyebrows rose until they almost met his hair; his mouth dropped open. It was not the best expression for a face as good-looking as his, she thought coldly, but then, what could you expect of a man who'd just learned that some Barbie dolls could actually walk and talk?

"You're kidding."

"I have no sense of humor when it comes to this kind of situation, O'Connell. Being dragged clear across the country on a wild-goose chase is not my idea of fun."

It had begun raining again, a slow, fine drizzle that left droplets of water glittering in Keir's dark hair. He ran his hands through it, which made it stand up in damp little tufts. He looked completely baffled. Cassie almost felt sorry for him...but then his expression went from baffled to disbelieving, and she remembered that the person who was getting shafted here was her.

"Let me get this straight," he said slowly. "You're here to interview for the manager's spot?"

She thought of telling him that she wasn't here to interview at all, that the job was already hers, but why bother? She was not staying. If she had to go to Boston or Hartford or all the way back to Vegas and wait tables sixteen hours a day, she was not staying here.

"Oh, I know. I know, O'Connell. How could that be? How could I have the audacity to think I could do anything more complicated than hustle drinks to the customers?"

"I didn't say—"

"You didn't have to." At least he had the decency to blush, she thought grimly, and she drew a deep breath. "I signed with TopNotch Personnel for a job managing a restaurant. They passed my résumé on to your Miss Davenport. She interviewed me over the telephone and hired me."

"Louise?" he said, with a laugh so infuriating she wanted to slug him, "*Louise* hired *you*?"

"You're repeating yourself again. I know how impossible it seems, considering my absolute lack of credentials. I mean, years of restaurant experience—"

"Restaurant experience," he said, with a smirk.

"Restaurant experience," she said, with an icy bite to

the words. "Something you'd know nothing about—unless you think strolling through the Desert Song's facilities and nodding at the help with that—that condescending look on your face constitutes experience?"

"I did not stroll through the Desert Song."

"No. That's true. Sometimes, you hung around long enough to bestow a benevolent smile on the peons."

"Nor was I condescending," he said stiffly.

"I guess not. You never asked any of us to bow."

Keir narrowed his eyes. "We seem to have gotten off track, Berk. You were explaining how you were able to con Louise into hiring you as her replacement."

"You mean, what lies did I tell?" Cassie smiled tightly. "Sorry to disappoint you, but I only told her the truth, that I'd put in years in the trenches." She paused for effect. "And that I have a degree in restaurant management."

Could a man narrow his eyes to slits and still see? Keir O'Connell could. At least, that seemed to be one of his talents.

"A degree in—"

"Restaurant management. Yes. I have a diploma I'd be happy to show you, *if* I were going to take this job, which I am not."

"Had it printed yourself, did you?"

"Oh, certainly." Cassie batted her lashes. "Right down at the corner Quik Copy. You'd love it. Great big gold seal, lots of curlicues..." Her sarcastic smile faded. "Listen, *Mister* O'Connell, not that our little chat hasn't been fun—"

"It isn't over yet."

"Trust me. It is." Cassie shuddered. Until now, fury at the thoughtless woman who'd brought her here, at the twist of fate that had shoved her into a face to face confrontation with this arrogant idiot she'd hoped never to see again, had warded off the cold. Now, she felt it seeping through her body, invading the marrow of her bones. If she didn't get warm soon, she'd turn into an icicle. "Maybe you haven't noticed, but we've nothing further to say to each other. Well, why would we? Emperors can't be bothered about the little people."

Keir unfolded his arms and put his hands on his hips.

"That's the second time you said something like that about me, Berk."

"My oh my. Hurt your feelings, have I?"

His face turned a color that reminded her of a plum sweater she'd once owned. He was angry. Really angry. It made her feel wonderful. Had he really gone through life thinking people didn't see right through that "I feel your pain, but we have to pull together for the sake of the team?" routine?

Okay. People didn't, but she did. She surely did. There'd been a time he'd had her fooled, too, but then she'd gone to that wedding...

"Sorry," she said sweetly. "You're right, of course. I didn't mean to repeat myself."

Keir dug his hands into his pockets and curled them into tight fists. She'd meant it, all right. Not that the taunt hurt. He never dealt with people the way she made it sound.

Hell, she was impossible. Gazing up at him from under her lashes...such long, thick lashes. How could a woman this beautiful be such a pain in the butt? Better still, how could she be so beautiful when she was as wet as a cat who'd just climbed out of a bathtub?

Wet? She was soaked. Anger had kept him from noticing it until now.

"You're soaked," he said.

"Really?" Cassie widened her eyes. "How clever of you to notice."

"How'd you get so wet?"

"It was raining, just like it's starting to do now. I guess it doesn't rain in your private world."

She unfolded her arms and put out a cupped hand, to

demonstrate. His eyes flashed to her breasts, clearly outlined under her wet clothes, and he felt a faint, unwanted tightening of his body.

"You look as if you stood under a waterfall," he said sharply.

"Close." She smiled thinly. "Now, if you d-don't m-mind—"

"Your teeth are chattering."

Dammit. They were. Nothing like chattering teeth to spoil the illusion of contempt she was trying so hard to maintain.

"Another astute obs-s-s-servation." She eyed him with defiance. "Goodbye, Mr. O'Connell. I won't say it hasn't been an in-in-interest—"

"Oh, for God's sake!" Keir reached out, scooped her into his arms. "By the time you finish the wisecrack, you'll be frozen solid."

"Put me down!"

"Believe me," he said, as he marched toward the office, "I intend to."

"Are you d-deaf?" Cassie pummeled his shoulders. "What did I tell you would happen if you t—touched me again?"

"You try to slug me, lady, you're in trouble."

"*I'm* in trouble? Did you ever hear of laws against k-k-kid—"

"Kidnapping," Keir said grimly, shouldering his way past the door. "Did *you* ever hear of hypothermia?"

"Give me a break, O'Connell. I—I—I'm not hy-hy-hy—"

"Yeah. Right." Keir carried her through the reception area, up the stairs and into his office where he elbowed the door shut and dumped her, unceremoniously, on her feet.

"Get undressed."

"What?"

"You heard me. Take off your clothes."

"In your dreams!"

He had to give her credit. Her teeth were chattering, her clothes were soaked and she bore more resemblance to a water rat than a woman—okay, a beautiful water rat, if there was such a thing—but she was still fist-in-your-face defiant.

He thought about telling her she'd gotten it right, that she *did* get undressed in his dreams, but what would that do except provide her with more ammunition?

"Give me some credit, Berk. If I wanted to get you into the sack, I'd try a more subtle approach. You need to get out of those wet things and into a hot shower. There's a bathroom behind that door. Wrap up in a towel when you're finished. I'll bring you something to wear."

"You're crazy."

"And you're dripping on the carpet."

She looked down. Water dripped off the tip of her nose and onto her soggy shoes.

"Have it cleaned," she said blithely, raising her eyes to his, "and send the bill to me. Now, s-step aside. I'm l-leaving."

Keir reached back, locked the door and leaned against it.

"I'm going to count to five, Cassie. Either your clothes are doing a disappearing act by then, or I'll just have to take them off you myself." He paused, his gaze fixed on hers. "One."

His voice was low, almost rough. He meant it; Cassie knew that he did. She thought about what it would be like if she held her ground, if she said yeah, fine, you just try it and see what happens, buster...

"Two."

And then she thought about how it would feel to have him open the buttons of her jacket, slide it from her shoulders. Thought about how he'd react when he saw what the rain had done to her sweater, how it clung to her breasts... Or had he already noticed?

"Three."

She could feel her nipples tighten. From the cold. Only from the cold.

"This is st-stupid," she said angrily, unsure if the anger was for herself or him.

"Four," he said, and started slowly toward her.

On the other hand, he wouldn't dare undress her. He was egotistical; he wasn't an idiot. Neither was she. To give an inch would be to lose not just the battle but the war.

Cassie folded her arms and raised her chin.

"Five," she said helpfully. "Six. Seven…"

He was inches away. A breath away. Neither of them was counting out loud but she could hear the numbers booming inside her head. Eight. Nine. Ten…

Keir reached out slowly, curled his fingers around the first button on her jacket, slipped it free.

"What the hell do you think you're d-doing, O'Connell?"

"Undressing you," he said coolly.

The next button opened, and the next. "Stop it!"

"I will." His voice was still pleasant but it had become low and rasping. His pupils were dark pinpoints as he slid his hands under her jacket, under her silk sweater.

She felt her head spin, felt desire course through her blood…

Cassie sprang back. Keir dropped his hands to his sides. They stared at each other for a long moment, his face taut muscle and bone, her heart pounding, and then he stepped back, too, and put even more distance between them.

"If you don't want me to do the rest, get into that bathroom and finish up for yourself."

He spoke calmly, looked at her calmly, as if nothing had happened. And nothing had—nothing, except that she was having trouble catching her breath and her skin tingled wherever his hands had been.

She swung away from him, because that was the only safe choice, and walked to the bathroom.

"Good girl," he called after her, and she turned, eyes flashing.

"I am not a g-girl, good or otherwise. Now, get out!"

"I'm going."

"My suitcase is in the t-trunk of my car."

"Fine."

"As soon as I get out of that shower and into a change of cl-clothes, I'm out of here."

"First you're going to explain why you flew 2500 miles for the chance to work with me."

The door clicked shut. Cassie glared at it. Then she kicked off her shoes and watched with satisfaction as they hit the wall and left thin smears of mud on the pristine white paint before falling to the floor.

A small victory, she thought as she turned the lock, but a victory just the same.

The shower felt wonderful.

She turned her face up to the hot water, then bent her head and let it beat down on her neck. After a while, she reached for the bottle of shampoo that stood next to the soap, opened it and took a sniff.

It smelled like lemon. Like Keir. His skin had a faint, lemony scent. Her brain must have registered that fact without her realizing it.

Cassie frowned, washed her hair, rinsed it, and picked up the soap.

It smelled like lemon, too.

Keir's shampoo. Keir's soap.

She'd been lathering her body. Now, her hand stilled. She looked down at herself, at her breasts, her thighs, at the translucent soap bubbles clinging to her skin.

Keir had used this same soap. He'd felt its soft kiss, its sensual glide and stroke...

"Dammit," she hissed, and dumped the soap back into its dish. Again, she lifted her face to the spray. This time, she adjusted the water until it was cool, let it beat down and clear her head. Once she felt like herself again, she shut off the water, wrapped herself in an oversize bath towel and cracked the door.

"O'Connell?"

No answer. She opened the door a little further and scanned the room for her suitcase. How long did he think it would take her to shower? Or did he harbor some funny idea about what would happen once she'd finished?

The man had a lot to learn. Didn't he think she'd learned anything from that day in Texas, to say nothing of that humiliating incident in the elevator?

The elevator. Thinking about it still made her cringe. At least he could have called and apologized, but no. He'd probably been too busy making jokes with his cretinous brothers at her expense—

The door swung open. Keir stared at her. She stared back. A feeling that was hot and electric shimmered in the air before she looked away.

"My clothes," she said briskly.

"*My* clothes," he said just as briskly, tossing jeans and a sweatshirt on the leather love seat. "They won't make a fashion statement, but they'll keep you warm."

"I want my own things, thank you."

"Yeah, and I want every table in my restaurant filled on the weekends. Why should I drag your suitcase up here when I'm only going to have to haul it back to your car when you leave?" He jerked his chin toward the stuff he'd brought her. "Go on. Get dressed."

Cassie's smile was all teeth. "What's the problem, O'Connell? Can't you make up your mind? First you want me out of my clothes. Then you want me in them." Holding the towel clutched between her breasts with one hand, she snatched up the jeans and shirt with the other. "As for the restaurant...try putting up a sign people can see and you might just pick up a customer or two."

"What?"

"Nothing," she snarled, and slammed the bathroom door in his face.

Keir took a deep breath. What was the matter with him? He'd seen half-naked women before. For that matter, he'd seen *this* woman half-naked before. That outfit, the costume she'd been wearing in the elevator...

He sank down on the love seat.

A man's head could explode, trying to get a handle on the real Cassie Berk. So far, he'd seen her dressed like a princess in a fairy tale, like a sex kitten, like a poor little orphan of the storm.

Now he'd seen her in a towel. No makeup. No fishnet stockings or take-me-I'm yours spiked heels. How could a towel be more provocative than those stockings and heels, than the skirt that had flirted with her backside?

It was, though. All he'd been able to think about was that under that towel, Cassie was all silky skin and warm, feminine scents.

His mouth thinned.

How many other men had thought the same thing? How many had tasted that skin, been surrounded by that warmth? He was making a fool of himself over a woman who'd pranced around damn near naked for half the men on the planet...

Except him.

And *she* was going to tell him how come his restaurant bookings were off? He laughed. Tried to laugh, anyway, though the sound came out more a snort of self-derision than anything else.

Okay. She'd caught him by surprise, that was the problem, turning up here, and on a bad day, too. Louise had caught him by surprise this morning, telling him she was leaving in a couple of hours. She'd promised to stay on a week, to break in the new manager...

Cassie Berk. The new manager. He groaned and leaned

his head back. Talk about improbable situations, that had to top the list. There'd even been a moment, standing in the rain, when he'd felt a tug of sympathy for her, coming all this way for a job that she'd never have, but so what? He had his own troubles. The vineyard was in great shape but the restaurant had a bucket of problems. Imagine handing it over to a woman whose closest connection to running a restaurant came from serving drinks to customers.

Okay. So she had some kind of management degree. It probably came from a diploma mill. Even if it didn't, he wasn't going to be her job-experience guinea pig. And he sure as hell wasn't going to get himself into a situation where the woman who'd been sashaying through his X-rated dreams shared his life, 24/7.

Keir rose to his feet, tucked his hands into his pockets and paced the room.

This was all Louise Davenport's fault. She'd seemed so capable, so easy to deal with, when he'd first bought Deer Run, but the more time had passed, the more temperamental she'd become.

None of the candidates she'd hired had worked out, either. He'd given her *carte blanche* in keeping with his policy of delegating authority, but not one of the people she'd taken on had made it through a week.

The last one had only lasted two days.

"I can't work with a slave-driver, Mr. O'Connell," the guy had said, just before he'd stomped off.

Slave driver? Him? Keir ran his hand through his hair as he sat down heavily in the chair behind his desk. He was the easiest boss in the world. Demanding, yes, but only of the best in people. He was never unreasonable, never unpleasant. Never.

"We've run out of suitable candidates, Mr. O'Connell," Louise had told him coolly, a week or two ago. "I'm afraid we're down to the last applicant."

Which brought him, full circle, to the woman in his bathroom.

No way. No way in hell would he—

The bathroom door opened. Cassie stepped into the room. This was better. His sweatshirt, his jeans, everything huge and hanging so that he wasn't distracted by the lush thrust of her breasts or the rounded curve of her hips.

"Satisfied?" she said coolly.

Keir waved a hand at the chair opposite his. She could be polite? So could he.

"Sit down please, Cassie."

Cassie sat. She must have used his dryer. Now that he thought about it, he'd heard its buzz through the closed door. Her hair was loose and hung straight down her back in a black fall of silk. The shower had washed away her makeup. She looked young, innocent, gorgeous...

Innocent? The last thing he'd done, before signing off at the Desert Song, was to pull her file and read it. She'd been a showgirl in glitzy Vegas extravaganzas. She'd danced behind a bar in a G-string, taken off her clothes for strangers.

Keir folded his hands and forced a smile to his lips.

"Well." He cleared his throat. "I must say, seeing you is quite a surprise."

"Why?" Her smile would have made an alligator happy. "Did you think they wouldn't let me cross the Connecticut border?"

She sat back and crossed her legs. They were the longest legs he'd ever seen.

"What you mean is, how did I end up getting hired by your sainted Miss Davenport."

A muscle knotted in his cheek. "Look, I'm trying to be polite about this, but—"

"But, you can't bring yourself to believe me." Cassie fluttered those long, impossibly thick lashes. "I'll bet you were hoping I'd say I'd come to find you," she said in a seductive whisper.

He felt the blood rush to his head and, dammit, to his groin. He didn't have to react when she baited him. She was good at that, even in his dreams. Sometimes he awoke, amazed that he hadn't ground his molars to powder during the night.

"Listen," he said, "here's the deal. I'll ask the questions, you answer them. Okay?"

Cassie shrugged one shoulder. "Fine with me."

Keir plucked a pencil from the desk. "Well," he said cautiously, "unless I misunderstood, you claim Miss Davenport hired you through the TopNotch agency."

"Wrong."

"Wrong?" Was there a glimpse of salvation on the horizon? "Then, TopNotch didn't…"

"They did." Cassie uncrossed her legs and sat up straight. The time for playing games was over. "And Davenport hired me."

"You mean, she asked you to come for a final interview" He clucked his tongue, shook his head, did whatever he figured it took to show some empathy "Well, what can I say. Cassie? I'm terribly sorry you were inconvenienced but—

"Do you have a hearing problem, O'Connell? She *hired* me. As in, she signed on the dotted line."

The pencil snapped and he tossed the two halves aside. "That's impossible."

"There's a contract in my purse that says it's not." Cassie smiled thinly. What the hell, why not give him a few minutes of suffering before she assured him she was leaving?

Keir's eyes narrowed. "Contracts are made to be broken."

"Really."

"Yes, really." He smiled, or tried to, and his voice took

on a conciliatory tone. "Look, I know you must be disappointed. And, I suppose, in a way, this is my fault."

"Is it?"

"Well, in the sense that I let Miss Davenport make some poor decisions." Wrong tack. He could see that in the way she raised her chin. She had a habit of doing that, he'd noticed, whenever he pissed her off. He sat back, steepled his fingers under his chin and tried another approach. "Tell you what. I'd like to be fair about this unfortunate situation. I'll pay your airfare back to Las Vegas."

God, the arrogance of the man. Did he think he could buy her off with an airplane ticket? Cassie smiled politely.

"Thank you."

His smile grew more congenial. "And, since you're being so understanding about this unfortunate error, I'll compensate you with a week's pay."

"How generous."

Keir felt the skin prickle on the back of his neck. Was there a warning in her voice?

"Yes," he said quickly, and pushed back his chair, "well, I'm glad we could resolve the matter so amicably."

"I do appreciate your admission of responsibility and your offer of compensation, Mr. O'Connell."

There was that prickle again. How come she'd suddenly started calling him Mr. O'Connell?

"No need to thank me," he said, even more quickly. "I'll just write you a check and—"

"But I'm not interested."

She spoke before she had time to think. Until this moment, she'd had every intention of walking. Defeat was preferable to working for a man like Keir O'Connell but who did he think he was, to try and buy her off? To sit there and look at her as if she were an insect that could be brushed away when it became annoying?

The man thought she couldn't run his restaurant. Well, he needed to be taught a lesson.

His smile fled in the blink of an eye. "What do you mean, you're not interested? It's a fair offer. More than fair. If you think you can hold me up—"

Better and better, Cassie thought coldly. She shoved back her chair and stood up.

"I'm staying, O'Connell. You wanted a manager. Well, you've got one."

"Don't be ridiculous. You can't—"

"Where's my apartment?"

"Your what?"

"My apartment. You know, the one that adjoins this building." Her smile was dazzling. "The one that comes with the job, fully furnished, rent free. Where is it?"

Keir shot to his feet. "Okay, I'm tired of playing Mr. Nice Guy. I have no intention of employing you. You don't know a damn thing about running a restaurant. There's not a way in the world I'd turn responsibility for Tender Grapes over to— Dammit, don't you walk out on me! Cassie! Where do you think you're going?"

"To get my luggage. Or a lawyer. Your choice."

"Dammit, Cassie—"

"I'd really like to get settled in before evening." She flashed a thousand watt smile that had as much warmth as a tray of ice cubes. "Despite what you think, I am fully qualified for this position. I'm sure the attorney I hire will tell you that. In the meantime, if you want me gone, you'll have to get the sheriff to evict me."

"Listen here, lady—"

"I really think you should consider your options," she said almost pleasantly. "I mean, the sheriff and a lawsuit would be bad enough, but the newspapers would just love a story about how the great Keir O'Connell tried to fire a woman who wouldn't succumb to his advances."

"What?"

"Especially in view of what happened in Texas."

He wanted to grab her. Wrap his hands around her throat. Turn her over his knee. Oh yeah, turn her over his knee...

"Think it over. Talk to my lawyer and try and hide from the press...or let me turn this place into a success." She cocked her head, waited. He didn't answer and she smiled. "Fine. That's what I thought. You've made the right decision, Mr. O'Connell. I'm sure you'll be delighted with the things I'll do for the Tender Grapes restaurant."

She walked past him, expecting him to grab her, expecting him to roar with fury but he just stood there, looking stunned. Stunned? Shocked right down to his toes, was more like it.

The Keir O'Connells of this world had a hell of a lot to learn about the Cassandra Bercovics, she thought grimly...and didn't let herself start to shake like a leaf in a windstorm until she was safely downstairs, trying to haul her suitcase out of the trunk of her car.

CHAPTER SIX

KEIR had the Irish gift of gab.

Mary Elizabeth O'Connell said that about all her sons and time had pretty much proven her right.

Sean had once talked his way out of a Marseillaise prison; Cullen had charmed his way into law school and Keir...well, a man didn't successfully head up a multimillion dollar resort without being able to navigate his way around a difficult situation.

Then how come he was standing in the middle of his office, as speechless as a ventriloquist's dummy, while Cassie Berk shot him a venomous look and then marched away?

The woman was trying to blackmail him. *Blackmail* him, by God!

"Hey!"

A brilliant comment, but saying something was better than standing here with his mouth open and his brain empty. Keir ran down the stairs. Cassie was already out of sight but how far could she go barefoot, wearing his jeans and shirt—and it was best not to think about how she'd looked in his clothes, because how she looked didn't have a damned thing to do with the fact that he'd sooner hire a pit viper than her.

The front door was open. He flew through it and reached her just as she leaned into the trunk of a small red Chevy.

"What do you think you're doing?" Getting her suitcase; that what she was doing. Trying to get it, was more like the truth. The damned thing was big enough to house a family of five. "Let go of that," he snarled, and grabbed her hands.

"Don't touch me, O'Connell!"

"You won't need your luggage. You can wear what you've got on. Nobody's going to give a damn about what you wear on that flight back to Vegas."

"I am not going back to Vegas," she said, grunting as she struggled to hang on to the handle of the suitcase and wrestle it from the trunk. "Damn you, get your hands off me!"

"You are not staying here, Berk. You're going to Vegas. Or to Siberia, for all I care."

"I am not going anywhere." Cassie tugged her hands free of his, straightened up and blew her hair out of her face. "I gave up my job and my apartment. I even sold my miserable car. I shipped the few things I couldn't part with here. What, precisely, am I supposed to go back to, huh? You know so much, maybe you know that!"

"That isn't my problem."

"Oh, but it is. Didn't I explain it clearly enough? You hired me. You want to get rid of me, you're going to have to fight me to do it."

She slapped her hands on her hips. A bad idea, Keir decided, because that tightened the loose sweatshirt he'd given her. Now he knew that she hadn't bothered with a bra.

Had she been wearing a bra before? Had she left it in the bathroom because it was wet, or didn't she ever bother wearing one? Why would a woman whose breasts were so high, so rounded, so perfectly suited to fit a man's hands wear a bra?

"Try listening instead of looking, O'Connell," she said coldly.

He looked up. Her voice was steady. There was a hint of color in her cheeks but he had to give her credit. She didn't flinch or fold her arms. Look all you like, she seemed to be saying; that's all you'll ever do.

Hell, *he* was the one who was blushing; he could feel the heat starting to rise in his cheeks, but why the hell should *he* be embarrassed, caught looking at what she'd let other men see a thousand times?

"I did listen," he said. "Now it's your turn. Get it straight, okay? There's no job for you here."

"I told you, I'll sue."

"Go ahead."

"Ah. I forgot. You've probably got Slimy, Sleazy and Scuzzball on the payroll."

He wanted to laugh, not at her but at the image that popped into his head of a bunch of oily legal eagles rubbing their hands with glee at the prospect of taking her on. She had a quick mind, he had to give her that.

"Actually," he said calmly, "I have something better." He paused for effect. "My brother's an attorney in New York. He'd like nothing better than to represent me."

"Oh, I'm sure." Cassie smiled politely. "Every lawyer just aches for the chance to get his name, and his client's, smeared across the front pages of the supermarket tabloids."

"Well," Keir said modestly, "I don't know about *every* lawyer, only about Cullen. Matter of fact, high-profile cases are his specialty."

"Do tell."

"Actually, he's just finishing a case right now that involves…well," he said, lying through his teeth, "I suppose it would be a breach of confidence to go into details, but you'd know the outfit, if I named it." He folded his arms and leaned back against the car. "Cullen sued a babe and her newspaper for defamation of character.

"And?" Cassie said, trying to sound bored. "What happened?"

"Cullen won and got a judgment against her and her newspaper for seven figures."

"Still," Cassie said, trying not to sound a little shaken, "all the negative publicity…"

"There's no such thing as negative publicity. You remember a while back, in Vegas, an actress caught her lover

in bed with...well, let's just say it wasn't your average in-
fidelity.'' Keir smiled again, with enough self-confidence to
make her teeth ache. "His next movie was a box-office
smash. Broke all records.''

Was it true? Was *any* of it true? The suit, the bad publicity being good publicity? She didn't know, wouldn't ask,
and wasn't going to be intimidated, either.

To hell with his smug smile. To hell with what he could
see outlined under her shirt. Let him look and eat his cold
heart out, because there wasn't a way in the world he'd
ever get to touch her again.

"Thank you for explaining it to me," she said sweetly,
"but I'll just have to take my chances.''

"Berk, have you actually heard anything I said?''

"I heard it all. I just don't how it applies to me. I mean,
what I have to lose? You want to sue me? Sue me. Your
brilliant brother could win a judgment of a trillion bucks
and it wouldn't matter a damn, once you saw my bank
balance. It's like I said. I have nothing to lose.''

"You'd accuse me of trying to blackmail you into my
bed?'' His face darkened. "You'd tell such a lie?''

"You don't know a damned thing about survival.'' Bit-
terness tinged her words. "If you did, you'd never ask me
that question.''

A muscle knotted in his jaw. She was good at this. At
coming on tough as nails and then, with a word or a look,
reminding him that she was a defenseless woman.

Well, hell, she was. He knew damned well she really
must have given up everything to come here, and even if
he was the coldhearted bastard she clearly took him to be,
that kind of thing only strengthened her case.

Not the one about sexual harassment. A good lawyer—
and Cullen was a terrific lawyer—could put a stake through
the heart of that *bête noir* without raising a sweat.

What he'd have difficulty beating was the simple fact that
Cassie had given up everything she had for a job he'd offered her. Sure, Louise Davenport had hired her, but Louise

was his employee. He'd ceded her the right to hire whomever she'd wanted, and she'd hired Cassie.

Check and mate. She'd won the game.

He just didn't have to let her know it.

Keir glowered at Cassie, tucked his hands in his pockets and paced toward the office. He could feel her eyes on him, burning against his back. Halfway there, he turned and paced back.

"Name your price. What'll it take to make you go away?"

A dozen possibilities flew through her mind. A month's pay. Two months. Three months. Why not? Despite the brother who was a lawyer, she had him over a barrel. He knew it as well as she did.

"I want what I was promised," she said. "The job as manager. The salary and benefits that go with it. The apartment, rent free."

Keir blinked. Back to square one, and with no way out. She hadn't backed down, not an inch. The lady had guts.

"I'll give you two months," he growled. "You screw up once in those eight weeks, you're history."

He saw the quick leap of fire in her eyes. She banked it just as fast, assumed a look that said she'd expected as much, but it was too late. She was happy. He'd made her happy.

It put a funny feeling in his gut. Discomforted, he glowered even harder.

"Are we agreed? Two months to prove yourself."

"Six."

"Three. One screwup and you're gone."

"Four, and some latitude until I'm familiar with your operation. That's my final offer, O'Connell."

He looked at her. Her chin was set at an angle that said she was prepared to battle to the end. Keir sighed and decided it wasn't worth it. Besides, who knew how long it would take him to find a manager—a real manager—to replace her?

"Four," he said. "One big-time mistake and you're toast."

"Fine, but we should agree on a definition of what 'big time' means." Cassie touched the tip of her tongue to her bottom lip. What was she doing? She'd bluffed her way into getting him to let her stay; why show nerves now? "For instance, dropping the salt shaker isn't a big-time screwup."

"No," he said coolly, "especially since we use salt mills. You do know what a salt mill is, Berk, don't you?"

There it was again, that nasty show of arrogance. Good. She could feel her confidence roaring back with a vengeance.

"I'm not going to dignify that with an answer, O'Connell. I just want to make sure we understand each other."

"Let me spell it out for you. You do anything to displease a customer, you're gone. Got it?"

Cassie nodded. "Got it." It was rude and crude time again. She could deal with that.

"Okay. That's it, then."

"No. Not quite. Two months' severance pay, should you fire me. Should you actually have *grounds* to fire me."

Keir nodded. "Agreed."

"And, despite this addendum to our initial agreement, you're going to keep to the rest of it. Pay my flight expenses, moving costs, provide health benefits—"

"You missed your calling. You should have been a lawyer. Slimy, Sleazy and Scuzzball would love you."

He was smiling. It was a joke, not an insult, so she permitted herself to offer a little smile in return.

"Hey, who knows? Now that I discovered school's not so bad..." She frowned and drew herself up. What she thought about school, or anything else, had nothing to do with him or their business arrangement. "It's been a long day, O'Connell. Mister O'Connell, I mean. If you'd show me to that apartment..."

"Keir."

"What?"

"Well, as you just realized, we can't call each other by last names if we're working together. And 'mister' and 'miss' won't sound right. Tender Grapes is a casual place."

"Casually elegant." His brows lifted and she flushed. "That's what Miss Davenport said. She said it was on the menu and on the letterhead."

"Well, she was right."

Keir moved slowly toward her. He had the grace and intensity of a big cat. Cassie wanted to take a step back but the car was right behind her. Besides, didn't all those wildlife programs say you should never show so much as a hint of fear to a big cat?

"Tender Grapes, Deer Run, our entire operation is casual but elegant." He shook his head. "Actually, I hate that word."

"Casual?" she said, a little breathlessly. He'd come to a stop inches from her, so close she could see that his eyes weren't really black but a deep, mysterious midnight blue. "Why? What's wrong with it?"

"Nothing. I mean, it's fine. 'Elegant' is the word I'd like to change. I'd prefer something a little more, I don't know, masculine." He reached out, touched his hand to her hair. "Your hair's getting wet again," he said softly.

Why was he touching her that way? Better yet, why was she reacting to it? His fingers brushed against her cheek and she felt the shock of his touch surge into her blood.

"How about—how about classy? Or—or chic? 'Casual but chic.' That would work."

"You're trembling, Cassie."

"The rain. It's the—"

"This drizzle?" He smiled, caught a strand of her hair between his fingertips. "I don't think so."

"O'Connell. Keir. I think we need to—to get something straight…"

"Yes. I agree."

He cupped the back of her neck with his hand. God, she was beautiful. He'd known lots of beautiful women, been involved with enough of them to know that women who looked like this and had spirit were rare. They were too egocentric to risk going toe-to-toe with a man. Women with looks that could send your pulse into the stratosphere purred to get what they wanted, or resorted to tears.

Cassie hadn't done either.

"Agree to what?"

To what. Yes, he remembered.

"You said we had to set something straight. And you're right. We need to clear the air, if this is going to work out."

Cassie drew a deep breath. If he wanted an apology for the way she'd forced his hand, he wasn't going to get one.

"I don't think we do. We reached a logical business agree—"

"I was talking about us."

"What 'us'? There is no 'us.' If you're referring to that— that thing in Texas, it was a mistake."

"Absolutely. It never should have happened…but it did. And I'm not going to lie to you, Cassie. There hasn't been a night goes by that I don't remember it."

He saw the pulse flutter in the hollow of her throat and he knew, *knew,* it was the same for her. The emotion that swept through him was all-consuming, hot, and dangerous. Better to deal with it now than later.

"Admit it," he said softly. "Tell me I'm right."

"You aren't! I can hardly remember Texas."

His eyes darkened. "You never give an inch."

"That's right. Never. And if that's what you hope will happen, that I'll bend—"

His mouth crushed down on hers. Startled, her hands flew up, pressed against his shoulders, but his arms went around her, drawing her hard against him, and all her good intentions scattered like fall leaves on a windy morning.

She moaned, a sweet, sensual message that went straight to his loins. Keir slid his hands into her hair, tilted her head back, kissed her relentlessly with a hunger born of endless nights and fitful dreams.

He didn't want her to bow. He didn't want her to bend. He wanted her as an equal, to play out the rest of their battle on soft sheets instead of sparring with words in a parking lot under the touch of a soft rain.

Her mouth parted under the pressure of his and he slipped his tongue between her lips, tasted her while she tasted him. He groaned and she wound her arms around his neck, lifted herself to him, wrapped one of those long, exciting legs around his.

God. To hell with sheets and beds. He was going to take her right here, against the car, pull down her jeans, drive into her again and again until they were both sated...

But a thread of sanity remained. He fought to catch it, to hang on to it. His hands dropped to Cassie's shoulders. He pulled back, and so did she.

He opened his eyes, looked into her face. Her color was high; her eyes were wide and unseeing. Her mouth was swollen from his kiss. And he—he was breathing like a man who'd just run a twenty mile marathon.

"We'll be working together," he said, his voice so thick that it sounded alien to his ears.

Slowly, Cassie nodded. "Yes," she whispered. "And that can never happen again."

"Agreed. That's why I kissed you. To get it out of the way." He cleared his throat, wondered if that sounded as ridiculous to her as it did to him. The trouble was, he meant it. Surely, kissing her would put an end to the wondering and the dreams. "From now on, it's strictly business." He let go of her and stepped back.

"Strictly business," she said, echoing his words.

He thought about holding out his hand. Then he thought about what might happen if she took it. Quickly, he reached past her for the suitcase.

"Well," he said briskly, "it's raining again."

"Umm. Yes." Cassie looked up as if the rain really mattered. "Does it always rain like this in Connecticut?"

Keir laughed and grabbed for the verbal lifeline. "Nah. When it gets really cold, it snows."

Cassie laughed, too, as if they'd shared a marvelous joke.

"Maybe you'd better show me to my apartment, before we drown."

"Right." He hoisted the suitcase from the trunk and slammed the lid shut. "You want to walk? It's only a couple of hundred yards but if you don't want to get any wetter..."

"A couple of hundred yards?" She shot a puzzled look past him, to the red barn that housed the office and reception area. "It's not even a hundred feet!"

Keir began walking briskly up the driveway. Cassie hesitated, then hurried after him.

"Keir? Where are we going? Louise said—"

"Louise said a lot things. As we're both finding out, most of them were wrong."

"She said the manager's apartment adjoined the office."

"The tasting room adjoins the office, and if you think I'm letting you set up housekeeping in a vat of chardonnay, think again."

"But—but the apartment... Where is it?"

"It's right there, in—"

The wind snatched up whatever else he'd said and flung the words away. Cassie tucked her hair behind her ears and ran to keep up. They were heading uphill, toward the handsome stone house with a turret she'd glimpsed on her arrival.

Keir opened the door and motioned her inside, but Cassie stayed on the top step as the wind tugged at her hair.

"Is this where you live?" When he nodded, she went down one step. "Forget it!"

Keir put down the suitcase. "It's not what you think."

"Ha."

"Listen, Berk, I'm cold and wet and tired of standing in

the rain, arguing with you. You want to come inside, fine. You want to spend the night curled up in your car, that's okay with me. I'll give you ten seconds to think it over and then I'm going inside and closing the door.''

''You're good at that 'I'll give you ten seconds' thing,'' she said furiously.

He grinned. ''Actually, it was five seconds the last time.''

''Dammit, this is not funny. I thought we just agreed—''

''One,'' Keir said calmly, ''two, three, four—''

Cassie called him a name that cast serious aspersions on his ancestry as she swept past him. He slammed the door behind her and tried not to wonder how she could look so bedraggled and so damned beautiful at the same time.

''Okay,'' she said, folding her arms and tapping her foot in a fast, angry rhythm, ''who gets to sleep on the sofa?''

''There is no sofa,'' Keir said calmly.

Cassie looked around. They were in a room that would have done a medieval king proud. An empty room, unless you counted the fireplace big enough to roast an ox, the suit of armor in the corner, and the wide stairs that swept up into gloomy darkness.

''I'm in the process of refurnishing.''

''Décor by Dracula, I'm sure.''

He laughed. ''That's the 're' part. I'm hoping to come up with something livelier.''

''Just make sure my sleeping bag's not on the same floor as yours.''

''No problem.'' He walked across the marble floor, his footsteps loud and echoing, took a key from his pocket and unlocked a door that was almost hidden behind the stairs. ''Your rooms, m'lady.''

Cassie hesitated. Then she strode past him and tried to keep her jaw from dropping. She was in a living room the size of her entire apartment in Las Vegas. There were other rooms leading from it. A bedroom. A kitchen. A bathroom...

"It's a little outdated."

The understatement of the century, but that didn't mean it wasn't handsome. Cassie stroked her hand over the back of a wine-colored velvet sofa, looked at the marble floor...

"What is this?"

"It's your apartment."

She spun around and stared at Keir. "Are you serious?"

"Just let me know what you need and I'll see to it."

He tossed an enormous brass key toward her, the kind that hung on the rings of diabolical housekeepers in scary movies. She snatched it out of the air.

"The lock's old," he said, "but it works."

"Even against vampires?"

Aha! The hint of a smile, the faintest suggestion of an olive branch. Keir smiled back.

"I'll just put your suitcase into the bedroom—"

"You stay the hell out of my bedroom, O'Connell!"

So much for olive branches. Keir started to say something, thought better of it, dropped the suitcase on the floor and stalked out.

CHAPTER SEVEN

KEIR stood at his office window, drinking coffee as he gazed out over the land.

His land.

After three backbreaking, exhausting months, he was starting to feel as if Deer Run actually belonged to him. Having your name on a deed was fine but putting your sweat into the soil was what mattered.

"Sweat equity," his old man had called it, the summer they'd had to spend rebuilding a falling-down cabin on a godforsaken lake in Arkansas. Ruarch had won it in a poker game and until his luck changed and he started winning again, the cabin and its leaky roof, stopped-up toilet and sagging floors were all they had.

"You'll love the place all the more, once you've put your backs into fixing it," Ruarch had told them, but it wasn't true

They'd all hated it, the girls for the mice that built their nests inside the old furniture, the boys for the never-ending work of trying to keep the structure from falling down around their heads. Only their mother had seemed happy, referring to the cabin as their place in the country instead of what it was, a miserable hovel on the shores of a lake that was home to an army of snapping turtles and water snakes.

Keir drank some more of his coffee.

He still despised the cabin, even in memory, but now he understood what his father had meant about sweat equity and the special feeling that could come with it when a man worked his hands raw on something that mattered to him.

Deer Run mattered.

Keir smiled ruefully. If he hadn't worked his hands raw, he'd certainly worked them hard. At Deer Run, workers harvested the grapes by cutting the heavy clusters from the vines at the exact moment they were ripe. Hand labor was costly and there were machines that did the job faster, but machines could damage the delicate fruit.

His vintner, a taciturn Californian from the Napa Valley, had expressed surprise when Keir showed up in jeans, sweatshirt and work boots the first day of the harvest.

"We have plenty of pickers, Mr. O'Connell," he'd said politely.

"It's Keir," Keir had replied, "and now we have one more."

After that, he'd worked side by side with the crew, picking grapes, unloading the heavy baskets into the pick-up cart, running the wine press and cleaning up at the end of each day. After a week, he knew more about grapes than he'd learned in the prior six weeks worth of reading and knew, too, that he'd passed some sort of subtle test when the vintner said if he wanted to learn about pruning and grafting, he'd be glad to teach him.

"Sure," Keir had said, as if the offer and his response were equally casual, but he knew damn well they weren't.

Now he felt as if he really owned these acres...or maybe they owned him.

Either way, it felt damn good.

He was happy, happier than he'd been at any job he'd ever held, and working harder than he'd ever imagined. Nights he spent at his desk in his office, writing up detailed plans for expanding the Deer Run market and reading everything he could about oenology and viticulture.

"Wine-making and grape-growing, for you ignorant beer drinkers," he'd told Cullen over dinner in Manhattan.

"Yeah," Cullen had said, "well, when you can appreciate the difference between a dark Bavarian ale and a good English stout, let me know." They'd grinned at each other.

"On the other hand," Cullen had added, "that bottle of red you sent me—"

"Merlot."

"That bottle of red," Cullen had said blandly, "wasn't bad."

They'd grinned again, talked some more, and then Cullen had mentioned, very casually, that he had a friend who was doing a feature piece for *The Times*.

"It's about people who've changed careers." Cullen had lifted his glass of Belgian White ale to his lips. "You think you'd be interested in talking with him?"

"Well… I don't think so. I'm too new to the business. I mean, I don't know a hell of a lot yet."

"Keir, are you nuts?" Cullen had pushed aside his plate and leaned over the table. "*The Times* must have a readership damn near big as the population of China."

"Yeah, but—"

"But what? You don't want all that free publicity? You don't want people in New York and most of the other civilized cities in the world opening the Sunday magazine section, turning to an article and reading about Deer Run vineyard and—what's the name of that restaurant?"

"Tender Grapes."

"Tender Grapes. Right. Which reminds me—did you ever find somebody to manage it?"

"Yes."

"And?"

"And, what?"

"And, how's the guy working out?"

Keir had thought of saying it wasn't a man, it was a woman, that it was, in fact, a woman Cullen had already met, however briefly, in an elevator in Vegas…

"Fine," he'd said, "just fine. So, tell me more about this friend of yours."

The upshot was that Cullen's pal had come to Deer Run. He and Keir had talked, a photographer had taken a couple of dozen shots and last weekend, the article had appeared in *The Sunday Times.*

There were a couple of paragraphs about the vineyard and only a brief mention of the restaurant. Keir had tried to point the guy toward it, asked him if he'd like to meet with his manager, but the freelancer hadn't been interested. It was the wine-making that had his attention. A 180 degree switch from Keir's prior career, he'd called it.

The piece had run with a photo of Keir standing on the highest ridge above the vineyard, looking out over his land.

Keir O'Connell's Kingdom, it said.

He'd taken a lot of teasing phone calls from his brothers and sisters, even one from Sean, on a yacht off the Côte d'Azur.

"Keir O'Connell's kingdom, huh?" he'd said, laughing, and Keir had pleaded ignorance.

"I never saw that title until the paper came out."

True…but that didn't mean he hadn't gotten a kick out of it. The phrase was presumptuous but it had a ring that he liked.

This place was his and nobody else's. The vineyards, the house, the restaurant. Whatever happened here, good or bad, would be the result of his hard work. Well, everything except what went on in the restaurant, which had turned into Cassie's kingdom.

Keir sat down, leaned back and folded his arms behind his head.

The day after she'd arrived, he'd walked her into Tender Grapes, introduced her to the surly chef and the now-you-see-them, now-you-don't staff. Cassie had said hello, how are you, pleased to meet you. The chef had grunted, the kitchen staff had shrugged, and the servers and busboys had given her looks that said why bother, when she wouldn't be around all that long.

"Listen up, people," Keir had said sharply. "I expect you to cooperate fully with Miss Berk. If you think you can't do that—"

"Thank you, Mr. O'Connell," Cassie had said with a big smile, "but I'm sure the staff and I will get along just fine."

Then she'd clasped his arm, hustled him to the door and, basically, tossed him out.

Later, when they were alone, she'd told him that if she ever needed any help, she'd let him know.

"I'll whistle," she'd said, without any pretence of a smile. "Until then, I prefer to establish a relationship with my people my way, and on my own."

"In other words," he'd said, "'thanks but no thanks,' and get the hell out of the way."

"You're a quick study, O'Connell," she'd said, and that was pretty much the last real conversation they'd had.

Keir sighed, pushed back his chair and put his feet on his desk.

He had to admit, she was doing her job. It was weeks since anybody had quit or the chef had brandished his meat cleaver. Food came out of the kitchen on time, empty dishes were promptly whisked away, the parking lot was almost full at every sitting...

...And his attempts at holding reasonable conversation were a flop. He talked. Cassie listened and said nothing, unless you counted "yes" and "no" as meaningful dialogue.

Amazing, how much meaning a woman could impart with words of one syllable.

Not that he cared.

What could they have to say to each other? Would she give a damn if he said, How was your day? How do you like New England? Were those really old phonograph records I saw in that carton when the moving guys were bringing in your stuff?

None of that was his business, not even what made her laugh, or if her throat tightened when she watched the sun dip behind the hills and the sky turned to flame.

Keir frowned and swung his feet to the floor.

Who gave a damn about any of it? Not him. Cassie Berk

was his employee. So far, admittedly to his surprise, she seemed to be doing a decent job. End of story. He'd made it a point to know a little about the people who'd worked for him in Vegas but if one of them had said, *You know, I get a real kick out of watching the sun set,* he'd have figured that person was nuts.

But then, nobody who'd reported to him in Vegas had the lovely face of an angel or the mercurial temperament of a cat. A sleek, green-eyed cat who could claw and hiss one minute and purr in your arms the next...

"O'Connell?"

Cassie was standing half inside the doorway and he knew the second he saw her that everything he'd just told himself was a lie. There were a hundred things he wanted to ask her, and not one of them had to do with business.

Flustered, he pushed back his chair and stood up. Damn, she was beautiful, even at this hour of the morning. What would she look like at this same time, in bed, after a long night of loving?

"Cassie." He cleared his throat. "Come in."

She took a couple of steps into the room, then hesitated. "If this is a bad time..."

"No, it's fine."

"Are you sure?" she said, and gestured toward the door. "Because if it's not—"

My God. She was being polite. A new leaf? A new Cassie? What was going on?

"Really, your timing's perfect. I was just, uh, I was thinking about you. About the restaurant, I mean. Please, come in and sit down."

She hesitated, then took a chair as he returned to his. He smiled politely and tried to figure out what in hell was happening. The only thing he could come up with was that she was quitting.

A couple of months ago, he'd have wanted to hear that. Not now. Whatever she'd done with Tender Grapes was working out. And even though their relationship was stilted—okay, even though they had no relationship—he liked seeing her, catching her floral scent in the entryway to the house, hearing the water run in his bathroom and knowing she was showering in hers, standing sleek and naked under the spray...

Stop it.

He cleared his throat, flashed what he hoped was a reassuring smile and folded his hands on the desk before him. "Well," he said briskly, "how are you settling in?"

"Fine, thank you."

Silence. He searched for another topic. "I noticed you're driving a different car."

"Yes. I returned the rental and leased a car instead."

"A good idea."

"I thought so."

More silence, and she was fidgeting. Well, why would he expect her to be at ease? They hadn't exchanged a pleasant word since he'd hired her.

"Cassie." What the hell. One peace gesture deserved another. "I want you to know that I'm pleased with the job you've been doing."

"Thank you."

Was he going to have to keep pulling conversational gambits out of the air?

"Well. What can I do for you this morning?"

He saw her throat move as she swallowed. "I—I need something."

"Really." That sounded polite, didn't it? "What?"

Cassie slicked the tip of her tongue across her bottom lip. She'd gone through this scene in her head at least half a dozen times, trying to envision it every step of the way, and she'd come to one, and only one, conclusion.

You could catch more flies with honey than with vinegar.

She'd used that approach to win over the restaurant staff. The brilliant but self-centered chef had stopped threatening to decapitate the almost-as-brilliant but painfully neurotic sous-chef, who'd stopped threatening to beat up the kitchen

workers, who'd stopped slowing things to a crawl. That
resulted in better service, which led to better tips, which led
to the servers and busboys not throwing off their signature
white aprons and stomping out the door.

All in all, what had happened was proof that textbooks
that emphasized the importance of getting along with those
who worked for you were correct. And that led, inexorably,
to the conclusion that the texts were equally correct in saying a successful manager found ways to get along with his
or her boss, even if that boss was an egotistical—

"Cassie? You were saying that you needed something...?"

Egotistical, and gorgeous.

All those days he'd spent, helping with the harvest.
Couldn't he have worn a shirt? It was unseemly, an employer going around like that, half-naked, his shoulders rolling with muscle, his chest lightly furred, the dark hair ar-
rowing down into his low-slung jeans.

"Yes." She smiled. He smiled in return, looking as innocent as a baby. "Yes," she said, "yes, I do."

He nodded, still smiling, but his eyes were wary. Well,
she could hardly blame him. She'd avoided him the past
two months, met each of his attempts at conversation with
all the warmth of a polar bear greeting a seal popping its
head through the ice, and now she was doing everything
but fluttering her lashes.

Stop it, she told herself sternly. You didn't need to be
Miss Congeniality to impress your employer. You could do
that with hard work. Besides, if she unbent too much,
O'Connell would let it go straight to his zipper.

"Well," he said, still smiling, "would you like to tell
me what it is you need?"

Cassie took a deep breath. "An advertising budget."

"Ah. An advertising budget."

He sounded wise and calm but she'd caught the tiniest
frown, as if he'd expected something else. Well, he wasn't
going to get it. One meaningless bit of chitchat, a little

remark about the old records she'd seen him eyeing when her stuff had been delivered or a comment about the incredible sunsets, and Mr. I-Am-God's-Gift-To-Women would figure she was cracking open the door to something far more personal, and why on earth would she ever do that?

Keir wasn't her type. She'd never liked men that were too good-looking, too big, too masculine, too everything. They did funny things to a woman's brain and, worse still, to her heart. Hadn't that happened with the miserable bastard who was her ex-husband? Her only husband, because he'd taught her a lesson about men and trust and love that she never wanted to learn again.

"For what kind of advertising? Have you thought that far ahead?"

Had she thought that far ahead? What he meant was, wow, amazing, that she was able to think at all. That was what most men thought, when they looked at her. How come she'd imagined Keir could be different? That he'd see there was more to her than a chance for fun and games?

Not that she wanted him to.

He was her boss, nothing more. So what if he lived right upstairs? There was no reason for her to think about him, or lie awake nights, wondering how come it was so late and he wasn't home, or try and figure out where he spent his time from Monday afternoons until Wednesday evenings?

She didn't care. Besides, it didn't take a genius to figure out why he wasn't at Deer Run Vineyard.

He was with other women.

Worse, he was probably with *one* other woman, somebody with that cool Connecticut look, long blond hair and an Ivy League accent…

Dammit, that wasn't what kept her awake nights. It was thinking of ways to improve business that made…

"Cassie?"

She jumped. "Sorry. I was, um, I was thinking about your question." She crossed her legs, uncrossed them when she saw his gaze drop to her knees, and brought them close together, feet flat on the floor, ankles touching. "I've given considerable thought to the kind of advertising I'd like to do."

"And?"

"And, I think we should start with an increase in our local print ads."

He leaned forward, elbows on his desk, fingers steepled under his chin, frowning as if he was considering running TV spots on the Zambian cable network.

"Well," he said slowly, "why don't you look into the cost, and—"

"I already have." Cassie placed a folder in front of him. "I've run the figures two different ways. They're on page three."

He frowned again, looked at her again, then opened the folder and bent his head over it.

"I see. Well, that's not too bad. Sure. Go for it."

"Which proposal? The first, or the second?"

"Oh," he said, with a magnanimous smile, "the second. What the heck, if you think it will draw business..."

"I'm sure it will. So will the proposal on page four."

"Page...?" He turned the page and read through it. When he looked up this time, his eyebrows were raised.

"That's very ambitious."

"I know. But we're booked solid almost every weekend, and we fill most of the tables Thursday and Friday, too."

"And?"

"And, I've identified our target market. Affluent. Well-educated. Mostly between the ages of—"

"I agree."

"Then, I'm sure you'll agree we have to make an effort to reach it."

"But we are reaching it. Didn't you just say we're almost 100% booked?"

"We could be 100% booked." Cassie leaned forward. "If we ran quarter page ads in some regional publications—'' She named two glossy, upscale magazines. "I've figured the cost."

"Expensive?"

"Yes. It's on the next page."

He turned the page, read it, then read it again. "More than expensive. Outrageous."

"Not when you consider the photo shoot and initial lay-out are one time costs."

"It's still a lot of money to spend."

"Not when you figure the return."

"The *possible* return."

"Look," she said, and stopped when she heard the first impatient note creep into her voice. With some difficulty, she forced a smile to her lips. "There's risk in everything, O'Con... Mr. O'Conn... Keir. I mean, you took a risk when you bought this place."

"A calculated risk. I knew what the land, the buildings, the label were worth. At the worst, I could have sold it for close to what I'd paid." Keir nodded at the folder on his desk. "This isn't the same kind of risk. I could spend all this money and get nothing for it."

"You ran ads for the Desert Song."

"That's different."

"How is it different?" Impatience tinged her voice again. "If you have something to sell, you have to let people know it's there."

"I will. I'm working on a plan, and—"

"I've already put a plan in front of you!"

"Cassie. I know you've given this a lot of thought but when you've had more experience..."

"Oh, for God's sake!" Cassie shot to her feet. "Would you do us both a favor and get that tone out of your voice?"

"What tone? Dammit, woman, I'm just trying to tell you something."

"That oily, self-righteous tone that says you're trying to educate me."

"Yeah. Yeah, I guess I am. What's wrong with that?"

"What's wrong is that you don't know the first thing about this."

"Give me a break, okay?" Keir shoved back his chair and stood up. "For six years, I ran—"

"For six years, you ran a hotel."

"A hotel with six restaurants under one roof!"

"Listen, O'Connell…"

"What happened to the 'mister'?" Keir shot back, his voice as icy as hers. "You know what your problem is, Berk? You can't keep a civil tongue in your head."

"You wandered through the kitchens at the Song like— like a general reviewing his troops."

"I beg your pardon?"

"You heard me. 'Hello there, Lester. How's the wife? How're the kids?'"

Her voice was pure female, but the intonation was a nearly perfect imitation of his. Keir felt heat rising in his face.

"And there's something wrong with that?" he said, as he came around the desk. "Come on, Madame expert. Tell me how you'd have done it."

"The same way, dammit. But this isn't the Song."

A sardonic smile curved his lips. "Congratulations on a brilliant observation."

"It's a small restaurant. You take a stroll through Tender Grapes, you could be in the front door and out the back in five minutes. Instead, you used to stand around for a hour, making everybody nervous because they couldn't decide what in hell it is you wanted."

"I was being friendly. It's a hands-on management technique. Something wrong with that?"

"In a little place like this, with a prima donna at the stove, yes, there's something wrong with it. It's not hands-on, it's in-your-face. That's how the chef saw it, anyway."

"What's the chef got to do with anything? The whole damn staff was out of control."

"A small restaurant operates like a game of dominoes. Upset one piece, the whole bunch collapses."

"Another incredible observation."

"It's a fact. You upset the chef all the time."

Keir folded his arms over his chest. "Name one."

"How about when you criticized the sauce for his New Orleans shrimp?"

"Criticized?" Keir shook his head, bewildered. "I simply said—"

"He told me how you hung over his shoulder, questioning his choice of ingredients, telling him how you thought he should make it."

"He's as nutty as you are. I never did anything remotely like that."

"You told him to use less butter."

"That's not true. I probably said something like, hey, no wonder that's so delicious, Henri, there's enough butter in there to clog an elephant's arter..." Keir frowned at Cassie's smug expression. "My God, it was a joke!"

"He didn't take it as a joke."

"He never complained."

"No," Cassie said coolly, "he just waved his cleaver in the air and snarled at the sous-chef, who saved face—"

"Excuse me?"

"The sous-chef is Chinese. Old country Chinese, in case you never noticed, and when Henri gave him a tongue-lashing, he turned right around and let it out on the salad boy, who—"

"This is a joke, right? A warped version of 'For want of a nail, a kingdom was lost'?"

Cassie's eyes darkened. "Do me a favor, O'Connell. Let's not talk about kingdoms."

"Huh?"

"I'll bet your Miss Davenport tried to tell you to stay out of the kitchen."

"Not true."

"She did. I can see it in your face."

Keir glared at Cassie. Louise *had* suggested he limit his visits, but what did she know about hands-on management? What did Cassie know about it? Nothing. Not one blessed thing.

And what made Cassie think she could ignore him for almost seven weeks and then come strolling into his office, first batting her lashes and then snapping off his head when he wouldn't do what she wanted?

What kind of fool did she take him for?

"We've gotten away from the point," he growled. "You want me to sink enough money to buy a small country into your hare-brained scheme. Well, I'm not going to do it."

"Okay. You want to talk about countries, we'll talk. Like the *Times* said, O'Connell, this is *your* country. Your kingdom, and why I was dumb enough to imagine you'd be open to advice on how to run it, I'll never know."

"I don't believe this. Are you annoyed because that article didn't mention you and the restaurant?"

Cassie knotted her hands into fists. "You know what, O'Connell? You're an idiot." She whirled around, stomped to the door, then swung toward him again. He was going to fire her. Why not go for broke? "Just for the record...doing the Nero thing, playing at being a farmer, isn't going to grow this place."

"It was Cincinnatus," he said, his voice dangerously soft as he moved toward her. "You're going to toss around Roman emperors, Berk, make sure you get the names right. And is that what you think I've been doing? Playing?"

She knew better. He'd worked as hard, maybe harder than anyone else, but she was angry as hell because he wouldn't listen to anyone else, because he wouldn't see that her ideas made sense...because he couldn't see that she was going crazy, working for him, passing him on the path from the house to the winery, wondering why he'd never tried to kiss her again...

"Yes. That's what I think."

Keir didn't answer. He came to within a breath of where she stood, his eyes hard, and her heart began to pound.

Maybe he was angry enough to kiss her. She hoped so, because it was time he admitted that was what this was really all about. It was why he snarled and she snapped. She was angry but her anger had less to do with his thick-headedness than it had to do with how badly she wanted him.

All these weeks, pretending she didn't. Who had she been kidding? Her job was wonderful, better than she'd ever imagined, but what kept her up nights wasn't the job.

It was Keir.

Why had she ever stopped him that night in Texas? She wanted him. In her arms. In her bed, and to hell with whether or not he'd respect her in the morning. She already knew the answer. He wouldn't. It was why she was all talk and no action when it came to men, but she didn't care anymore. She wanted Keir, wanted him, wanted him—

"You know what you need, Berk?" he said softly.

Her mouth was as dry as the Nevada desert. "Do you?"

"Yes." His voice roughened, and she could feel her heart trying to leap from her breast. "You need a lesson, and I'm the man to give it to you."

"Keir." His name came out a whisper. "Keir..."

"What time does lunch finish up?"

She blinked. Sex by appointment? "Four, but why do you—"

"Good." He turned away, went to his desk and reached for the phone. "Be ready to go at five-thirty."

Cassie sagged against the door jamb. He wasn't taking her to bed, he was firing her.

"Five-thirty, Berk, you got that?" His eyes flickered over her. "Change into something a little dressier."

She stared at him. "Change into..."

"Something dressier." His expression was unreadable. "Nothing, uh, frilly, just something you'd wear to an expensive restaurant. You do have something like that, don't you?''

Her brain was stuck on one track. "You're not firing me?"

"For speaking your mind?" His smile was thin as a razor. "I know you think I don't know the first thing about managing people but I can assure you, whatever else I am, I'm not in the habit of firing people for being honest." Keir reached took the receiver from the telephone. "Five-thirty. Please be prompt."

Be prompt? Wear something dressy? She'd come in here with a plan she'd spent days developing. He'd not only rejected it, he'd scorned it. Then he'd let her think he wanted to make love to her—that damned well *had* to have been deliberate—and now he told her, *told her,* that they were going out on a date?

Arrogant didn't begin to cover it.

"You're joking."

Keir raised an eyebrow. "I never joke about business. You think I've been neglecting Deer Run. That I'm living out a rich man's fantasy, digging in the dirt." His eyes narrowed. "Well, you're wrong."

"Look, O'Connell, I don't really care whether or not—"

"Yeah. You care, because your job depends on what I do, or don't do, with this place." A muscle knotted in his jaw. "I know you don't approve of my management style but hands-on is the way I go, Berk."

"I have no idea what you're talking about."

She was angry and puzzled. He could hear it in her voice, see it in her eyes. Good. Did she really think she could waltz in here and accuse him of not knowing how to run his business? Of being a dilettante? Did she think a steamy look would get her what she wanted, or maybe set him up for more humiliation?

The woman figured she could read him like a book, and it was time to change that perception.

"Let me spell it out," he said curtly. "We're taking a little educational tour this evening. Why not save whatever else you want to say for then? It's a two hour ride into Manhattan." Again, he flashed that thin smile. "Why spend it in silence?"

"It's a three hour ride," Cassie said faintly. "Almost four."

"Two, when I do the driving." He hesitated, not wanting to ask, knowing he had to. "How do you know how long a drive it is?"

"I drove down last week."

His eyes met hers. "Do you know someone in New York?"

She'd gone to a seminar on wine-making that she'd seen advertised in a magazine, but that was none of his business.

"I know a lot of people," she said, doing her best to sound offhand about it.

His mouth twisted. "How nice for you." He nodded to the door, the gesture bluntly dismissive. "Five-thirty, sharp."

"What if I say I don't want to go?"

"That's easy." This time, his smile was real. "I'd do what you expected me to do a couple of minutes ago. I'd fire you, and I'd smile while I did it."

A string of epithets that surely described such an insufferable man flashed through her head but she wasn't a fool. Keir O'Connell made promises, not threats.

"Yes, sir," she said crisply. "Five-thirty, sir, and in proper uniform. Sir."

"Now you've got the hang of it," he said, and watched with grim pleasure as she turned color, spun on her heel and flounced out of the room.

CHAPTER EIGHT

CASSIE looked around her bedroom and wondered if it qualified as a disaster area, or just as proof that she was certifiably insane.

Neatness counts.

She'd grown up whispering that mantra. It was something you learned early, when your mother was too drunk to notice that there was a week's worth of dishes in the sink.

Once she was on her own, she'd even thought she obsessed about being neat and she'd forced herself to let a glass languish on the counter before washing and drying it, let a blouse hang on the back of a chair awhile before putting it into the laundry hamper.

Cassie took another look at her bedroom and rubbed her hands over her face.

If a herd of buffalo had gone through the place, could it really look any worse?

Clothing was piled on the bed; shoes were strewn across the floor. Panty hose in three different colors hung on the lampshade and the few pieces of jewelry she owned lay on top of the old-fashioned dresser.

She shot a frantic look at her watch.

Five o'clock, on the nose. Half an hour to go and she'd already wasted forty-five minutes trying on and discarding her entire wardrobe.

Nothing frilly, just something you'd wear to an expensive restaurant. You do have something like that, don't you?

Nice. Really nice. Translation: He didn't want her to wear anything that would embarrass him. No feathers. No sequins. No tiny little skirts or fishnet stockings. Nothing that would better suit a bump-and-grind than his exalted company.

Cassie sat down on the edge of the bed.

Too bad she'd tossed out all her cocktail waitress outfits before moving east. Too bad time travel didn't exist so she could go back to Vegas in the year she'd worn that Eiffel Tower costume and bring it here.

Smiling, she sat back, crossed her legs and waggled one foot back and forth.

Oh, how she'd love to do that. Wear the rhinestone-trimmed demi-bra and the thong panties with gold fringe. Put on that ridiculous headdress. Yes, it looked as stupid as hell but the apparatus that held it up made you keep your shoulders back, way back unless you wanted to topple over, and that made your boobs stick out in front of you like two ripe cantaloupes. And don't forget the see-through plastic shoes with heels high enough to be declared lethal weapons.

Cassie chuckled. Too bad. If only such a thing was possible. Then, in just about—she checked her watch—in just about twenty minutes, she could watch Keir O'Connell take one look at her and fall flat on his handsome face...

Twenty minutes?

Her blood ran cold. "Ohmygod," she said, and leaped to her feet.

The truth was, she didn't have anything that was 'dressy.' She'd spent a small fortune on a couple of classy suits, some blouses, a handful of dresses, all of them designed to make her look like what she figured a lady manager was supposed to look like, but dressy? Not in O'Connell's book. She'd seen him at the Song in his made-to-order suits, at Dawn's wedding in his made-to-order tux.

Cassie blew her hair out of her eyes as she pawed through the clothes on her bed.

Everything the man wore was made-to-order, probably including his pajamas. If he wore pajamas. Did he? Or was there nothing between that hard, leanly-muscled male body and the cool softness of the sheets?

Cassie frowned.

Who cared what he wore to bed? For that matter, who cared what she wore tonight? Why was she tearing through all this damned clothing a second and third time?

Neat and tailored would do fine.

Ridiculous, all this worry over what to put on. She was behaving exactly like Dawn when she'd dressed for her first evening with Gray.

This isn't a date, Dawn had kept saying, even as she said "no" to one outfit after another. She'd been wrong, of course. It *had* been a date...

Cassie scowled, put her hands in the small of her back and straightened up.

Yes, but this wasn't. It was a command performance. *Big* difference! Dawn had been shaking with excitement, even as she'd denied it. She'd already fallen for Gray; she just hadn't wanted to admit it.

Cassie went to her closet and looked inside, though there was little left on the hangers.

She certainly wasn't shaking with excitement. Neither had she fallen for Keir. Oh, maybe she got a little rush sometimes, looking at him, but a woman would have to be dead not to react to a man like him.

Besides, she wasn't stupid. What would be the sense in falling for a guy who wanted no part of you?

Only one suit remained in the closet, a black silk. The skirt was short and straight; the jacket had a mandarin collar and tiny jet buttons all down the front. The suit was elegant and ladylike but buying it had been a costly mistake. It was businesslike, yes, but a bit dressier than...

Of course! It was perfect.

She tore the suit from its hanger and tossed it on top of the heap on the bed. She'd keep the jacket closed but she had a crimson silk camisole somewhere... There it was. She'd wear it in the event the suit felt too warm and she wanted to open a couple of buttons. Add some off-black panty hose and a pair of black pumps with a nice, sensible heel… Excellent. Not even Keir O'Connell could—

Cassie paused. One pair of shoes remained in the closet, crimson suede pumps cut low in the front and with a slender, almost-but-not-quite-lethal heel. She'd bought them on the spur of the moment because they were on sale and gorgeous. They were also impractical, which was why she'd never worn them and probably never would, even though they'd look wonderful with the silk suit, especially if she actually left a couple of buttons undone on the jacket so the camisole showed.

If this were a date, that's what she'd wear. But it wasn't a date…and she was cutting it awfully close. Her watch said she had eleven minutes to go.

Not a problem. Years of making costume changes at the speed of light meant she could get completely dressed in the time it took other women to put on their underwear.

Underwear.

Cassie paused as she pulled on her panty hose. She hated panty hose. They were never long enough, no matter what brand she bought. An hour from now, these would undoubtedly be sitting down around her hips.

She glanced at the black silk suit.

For years, she'd worn a garter belt and stockings but she'd given that up when she made her career change. Demure suits and dresses seemed to call for panty hose, no matter how uncomfortable, no matter that nobody knew what she was wearing under her clothes.

A garter belt would be so much more comfortable.

A red silk garter belt, like the one in her underwear drawer. Now that she thought about it, she'd bought the shoes and the belt on the spur of the moment, right before she'd gone to Dawn's wedding. Who had she bought them for? A woman didn't buy stuff like this for herself, she bought it for a man…

Cassie frowned, pulled on the panty hose and everything else, added a touch of light makeup, discreet gold hoop earrings, a slender gold bracelet, and turned toward the full-length mirror on the bathroom door.

She looked fine, from every angle. Attractive. Professional. Elegant.

She'd still look elegant if she swapped the sensible black pumps for the red suede.

Yes, but Keir…

Keir? Keir was her boss. He wasn't in charge of her life. If he didn't like the shoes, who cared?

"You manage the vineyard, O'Connell," Cassie said, "not me."

Saying the words was wonderful. Acting on them was even better. She kicked off the practical black shoes, reached for the red ones, paused…

Her watch read five-seventeen. Her heart was racing. No. It was silly. It was pointless.

It was what she wanted to do.

Cassie hiked up her skirt. Off with the panty hose, on with the garter belt and sheer black hose. What I-Am-God O'Connell didn't know couldn't hurt him, and there wasn't a way he'd ever know about the belt.

A tremor sizzled along her nerve endings like a flash of lightning.

Not a way in the world would he know about the belt.

"In for a penny," Cassie whispered. She grabbed a red lipstick, ran it over her lips, and flew out the door.

How long did it take a woman to get ready to spend an evening with a man?

No, Keir reminded himself as he paced the entry foyer, that was poor phrasing. This wasn't a date. Not by any stretch of the imagination. This was a business meeting and when it was over, the lady with the fast mouth and the nasty accusations would know just how wrong she was.

Playing, huh?

Keir paced faster.

Was that what she thought he'd been doing? Days out

among the vines, nights buried in textbooks, weekends spent shaking hands and talking until his throat was sore, convincing *sommeliers* and restaurant owners to buy his wine? That was play?

He'd been working his tail off while Cassie did a stint as amateur shrink to a chef with an attitude problem. Oh, yeah. *That* was definitely hard work.

No wonder she'd driven into the city to unwind, doing who knew what with who knew whom.

He'd have to talk to her about that. Certainly, she was free to do as she wished on her own time but Manhattan was almost 200 miles from here. She would have to understand that she couldn't make the trip when she had to work the next day.

Keir's scowl deepened.

Actually, he'd tell her she wasn't to make the trip at all. She was his manager. She had to be on hand in case she was needed. That wasn't asking much, not if she was serious about her responsibilities...

"I'm ready whenever you are."

"About time," he grumbled as he turned toward her. "I said five-thirty and it's almost five thirty-thr..."

Holy hell.

Dressy, he'd told her. And she'd complied.

Keir stared at the incredible vision in black and red. Words ran through his head. Stunning. Elegant. Demure.

And sexy. Sexy enough to start the blood draining from his head, straight into the part of his anatomy that least needed it. Everything about her screamed "woman" in capital letters.

That gorgeous hair, streaming over her shoulders. The spectacular face. The tiny hit of red peeking out of the half-buttoned jacket. Those long, endless legs...

And those shoes. Man, those shoes.

How was he ever going to get through this night?

Getting his jaw off the floor might be a good start. So

would breathing. Lack of oxygen only made an already bad case of ZTS worse.

Keir cleared his throat, worked up a scowl because only a scowl felt safe, walked past Cassie to the door and opened it.

"You're late," he said gruffly, "and we have appointments scheduled."

Was that a quick flash of disappointment he saw? Probably. She must have figured she'd knock him off balance, looking the way she did, but that wasn't going to happen. He was her employer. She was going with him tonight so he could teach her to think before she spoke...

Except, there were a thousand other things he wanted to teach her, and not a one of them had to do with how to run a restaurant.

It was going to be one very long night.

Keir had said they'd talk in the car, but they didn't. Cassie didn't care. She had nothing to say to him and besides, why would a woman talk to a man who so obviously resented her presence?

She shot him a quick look.

Actually, there were some things she might have said, asked him, anyway, had he given her the opportunity. Where, exactly, were they going? Manhattan, he'd said, but what did that mean? What kind of "appointments" had he scheduled?

Mostly, though, the questions she'd have asked were none of her business, like, did he always drive so fast? They might as well have been in a rocket hurtling through space.

And why had he become so angry at the sight of her?

Well, really, she didn't have to ask.

Cassie glanced down, then chewed on her lip. Foolish, to have worn the red shoes and the camisole. Her temper had gotten the best of her. Okay, so she'd made a mistake. She couldn't do a thing about the shoes but she could do something about the camisole.

SANDRA MARTON   113

She looked at Keir again, to make sure his attention was
still fixed on the road. He had on a dark gray suit, white
shirt and red tie; he'd tossed a black raincoat into the back
of the car, which reminded her that she'd gone out the door
without so much as a jacket.

If she froze into a block of ice he'd probably be annoyed
because he'd have to handle her with tongs.

She glanced at him again. Such a stony profile. Such a
hard-set jaw. Such rugged masculinity.

How could he look so angry and still look as sexy as
sin?

"What?"

Blood swept up under her skin as he turned toward her,
his eyes cold, his tone rapier sharp.

"What, what?" she said, and almost groaned at how stupid she sounded.

"You keep staring at me."

She felt her blush deepen. "Don't be silly. Why would
I stare at you?"

"That's what I'm asking. Is there something you want to
say?"

"Not a thing."

He made an unintelligible grunt and turned his attention
to the road. Cassie waited until she was sure he'd forgotten
all about her again. Good. She didn't want him to see her
closing the little jet buttons. He was egotistical enough to
think she was doing it out of deference to his Puritanical
tastes.

Slowly, working from the bottom up, she began easing
the buttons through their loops. One. Two. Three...

"Leave them."

Cassie jumped. Keir's voice was harsh and he was looking right at her.

"I'm just—I thought I'd close—"

"You look fine the way you are."

Fine. Not beautiful. Not seductive. Just "fine," spoken

with less emotion than he might have shown complimenting the sous-chef on a dish of vegetables.

She made a little sound, covered it with a cough and folded her hands in her lap. What in the world was wrong with her tonight? Fine was good. It was perfect.

It was all she wanted.

The car filled with heavy silence and stayed that way until they pulled up in front of a discreetly lit doorway on the East side of Manhattan. A large man in a maroon jacket stepped off the curb and went around to Keir's side of the car.

"Good evening, sir. Tonight's password, please?"

Cassie raised her eyebrows. "Amazonia," Keir said, handing over his keys.

The man grinned. "Yes, sir. Welcome to Lola's."

Lola's? Secret Passwords? More games, Cassie thought, as she stepped onto the curb and studiously ignored Keir's proffered hand.

Walking through the door was like walking into another world. The club, small and dark, pulsated to a DJ's heavy, electronic mix. Trees rose all around the room, vines curled around their trunks, leafy branches lifting to form a dense rainforest canopy. The air was warm and humid; water from what looked like a high waterfall tumbled endlessly beyond the raised, mirrored dance floor.

"It's a private club," Keir said, bending his head to Cassie's. "Very exclusive. And expensive."

Was she supposed to be impressed? Cassie smiled politely. "That's nice."

"Dammit, Berk, it's not 'nice,' it's—"

"Keir!"

A woman with copper skin, brilliantly blue eyes and the exotic look of a jungle cat, flung herself into Keir's arms. He grinned and kissed her lightly on the mouth.

Cassie watched with a polite smile on her face. Wouldn't it be fun to peel the woman off him, like the skin on a peach? An overripe peach. Under all that makeup, she had to be forty.

"Lola. You're beautiful as ever."

Forget forty. More like fifty, and weren't those little suture scars under the lady's eyes?

Lola turned her pale gaze on Cassie, almost as if she'd heard her thoughts.

"And this is…?"

"Cassie. Cassie Berk."

"Ah." Lola smiled politely. "Very nice," she said, as if Cassie weren't there.

"Cassie works for me."

Cassie works for me. Well, of course. He'd have to be sure Lola understood the arrangement.

Lola held out a languid hand. Cassie smiled through her teeth and shook it. Who was this woman? Was she the reason Keir left Connecticut Monday afternoons and never returned until Wednesday nights?

"Nice to meet you," she said politely.

Lola grinned. "Is it really?"

Keir cleared his throat. "Do you have a table for us? We can't stay long, so if you need to tuck us into the back of the room, that's okay."

"You? In the back of the room?" Lola linked her arm through his. "Nothing but the best for you, *querida.* Come with me."

She led them past tables packed with people Cassie recognized from the glossiest magazines, to a tiny table near the raised dance floor. A placard that said "reserved" stood centered on the tabletop. Lola whisked it away, insisted they sit down, gave Keir another of those butterfly kisses and paused beside Cassie's chair. She bent down and put her lips close to Cassie's ear.

"Save those murderous looks, little girl. I'm not sleeping with him." She gave a throaty laugh. "Not that I haven't tried."

"Really?" Cassie raised her voice to be heard over the music. "I couldn't care…" The music paused. "…less."

The word emerged a shout. Keir looked her with curiosity and she felt color stripe her cheeks. "I work for Mr. O'Connell," she muttered, as the sound picked up again. "That's all."

Lola chuckled and straightened up. "I hope your Miss Berk is a better manager than she is a liar, *querida.* I'll send Carlos over right away."

Keir waited until the crowd swallowed Lola. Then he leaned forward.

"What was that all about?"

"What was what all about?"

"The little cat session."

"What cat session? I don't know what you're talking about."

"Give me a break, will you? You and Lola were glaring at each other."

Cassie gave what she hoped was a negligent shrug. "You're seeing things that aren't there, O'Connell. Why not get down to business, instead of trying to read tea leaves? Why'd you bring me here?"

Why, indeed? This morning, taking her with him while he dropped in on a couple of the places where it had been the most difficult to add Deer Run Vineyard to the wine list had seemed a clever plan. Now, he couldn't imagine why he'd thought so.

What was that perfume she was wearing? Its fragrance teased his nostrils. And what about that bit of scarlet peeping out from under her jacket? Was that lace? Was that the shadowed hint of cleavage?

Was he losing his sanity?

"Listen," he said gruffly, "I've been thinking it over and—and I think we should call it a night."

Cassie blinked. "Already?"

"Yes. Yes, I really think—I think—" He drew a deep breath. "What do you call that thing you're wearing?"

"What thing?" She watched his eyes drop to her camisole, then rise to meet hers. "Oh." Cassie folded her hands tightly in her lap. "Uh, it's a camisole."

"A camisole." A muscle tightened in his cheek. "It's—it's very attractive."

Very attractive? A silk camisole, hand-trimmed in lace, was attractive? Dawn had given her the camisole as a birthday gift last year. She hadn't wanted to accept it; she knew it must have cost a small fortune, but Dawn had insisted.

"I want you to have it, Cassie," she'd said. "It's perfect for you."

But not perfect enough for her boss, Cassie thought, and smiled politely.

"Thank you."

"Yeah. I mean, you're welcome. I mean..."

Hell. What *did* he mean? Definitely, it was time to turn the car around and take her home. Or take her to bed. One or the other, before he exploded.

"Cassie. Cassie, listen..."

"Ah, there you are. Lola told me you'd just come in. Good to see you, my friend."

Saved by the bell, Keir thought, and rose to his feet.

"Carlos." He held out his hand to a tall, handsome man. "How are you?"

Carlos grinned at Cassie. "What he means is, have we sold much Deer Run wine."

"Oh. Sorry. Cassie, Carlos Rivera. He's Lola's wine buyer. Carlos, this is Cassie Berk. She manages my restaurant."

"Of course. Tender Grapes." Carlos took her hand and brought it to his lips. "I'm happy to meet you, Cassie. Keir's told me what a great job you've done."

Was her mouth hanging open? Cassie shot a look at Keir. His expression was noncommittal.

"Has he? Well—well, thank you."

"How lucky for you that you don't have to plead for more bottles of *vino* from the boss." Carlos pulled out a chair and sat down. "We sold out, Keir. Not a bottle of any kind left."

Keir sat back and smiled. "Yeah?"

"Yeah. That order I placed with you? Double it."

Keir was grinning like a kid who'd just found out he was getting a puppy for his birthday.

"When I think of all the fast-talking I went through to get you to give us a try…"

"I'm glad you did. Your wines are excellent." Carlos turned to Cassie. "So, Cassie. Your accent tells me you're not from this part of the country."

"Yours tells me the same thing."

Carlos grinned. "Bright, as well as beautiful. Keir, you have excellent taste in women."

"In employees," Keir said in a stiff tone. "She works for me, remember?"

"Of course. And I am happy that she does." Carlos glanced toward the dance floor. "Then you won't object if I ask her to dance?"

"Oh," Cassie said quickly, "I don't think—"

"Ask her, by all means." Keir's voice had gone from stiff to rigid. "The lady's free to do as she wishes."

Cassie looked from Carlos to Keir. Keir's eyes were flat and expressionless. It was the way he'd looked at her for far too long. Far too long, she thought, and she beamed a smile at Carlos and pushed back her chair.

"In that case," she said brightly, "the lady would love to dance."

Carlos rose and held out his hand. Cassie started to take it, then paused.

"Wait just a minute…" Quickly, she undid the rest of the buttons on her jacket, slid it off and took Carlos's hand. "Let's go," she said, and smiled.

For the second time that night, Keir almost forgot to breathe.

Yes, the camisole had a delicate ruffle of lace. Thin straps, too. And yes, Cassie's breasts, just their lush curve, swelled delicately above the lace. One of the straps slipped off her shoulder as she followed Carlos up the steps to the dance floor. Each time it did, she reached up to touch it and, dammit, that simple little gesture was turning him hard as stone.

He was going crazy here.

The music was hot and fast. Cassie faced Carlos and began to move.

Keir's throat tightened. Lord, could she move.

She was graceful. Sensual. Sexual. She was the essence of everything female, and he wanted to go up the steps to the dance floor, pull her into his arms and carry her into the darkness of the night.

He wouldn't, of course. He'd vowed not to repeat that one-time mistake. Okay, that two-time mistake. Besides, this was a public place. If-*if* he ever tried to kiss Cassie again, he'd wait for a quiet, private moment.

Cassie raised her arms in a graceful arc that lifted her breasts. She shook her bottom, tossed back her hair and laughed as Carlos leaned in and said something.

Keir pushed his chair back an inch.

Kiss her? Hell, he wouldn't stop at kissing her. He'd devour her, bury himself in her, take her to his bed and keep her there until they were both sated, except he couldn't imagine sating himself on Cassie. With Cassie. Couldn't imagine himself wanting to stop making love to her.

Carlos moved closer, smiling. Smiling and dancing, his hips moving, his body an inch from Cassie's, and Keir said a short, ugly word and exploded from his seat.

He snatched up Cassie's jacket and tiny purse, shouldered his way through the dancers and grabbed her hand. He swung her toward him and saw her eyes widen, saw Carlos look at him as if he'd lost his mind, but he didn't give a damn.

"Keir?"

"We're leaving."

"Leaving? But why?"

"Because I said so. That's why."

"Keir," Carlos said, *"meu amigo..."* He raised his hands, palms out. "I asked, didn't I? And you said—"

"It's not your fault," Keir said sharply. "It's not anybody's damned fault but my own."

"Keir." Cassie tried to tug her hand free of his. "Keir, what are you doing? I'm not leaving until you tell me—"

"Yes," he said, "you are."

She cried out as he pulled her against him and took her mouth with his. She fought him at first, beating her fists against his shoulders, and then she shuddered, whispered his name, and kissed him back.

The crowd erupted in a wild roar but Keir didn't hear it. All he could hear was the beating of his heart, all he could see was Cassie's upturned face, her parted lips, her heat-filled eyes as he held her tightly in the curve of his arm and led her into the night.

CHAPTER NINE

MANHATTAN'S concrete and glass canyons blazed with light but within moments of leaving the city, night embraced the speeding Ferrari.

Keir had discovered a route that consisted of a series of back roads that wound between the city and Deer Run Vineyard. He hadn't taken it driving down tonight because it wound sinuously through overgrown forests and hairpin turns.

It was the way he'd chosen to return home.

Every mile, every minute, counted.

Beside him, Cassie sat silent, her hands folded in her lap. Was she having second thoughts? Did she regret letting him all but carry her out of Lola's? Had he made a mistake putting close to two hours, two endless hours, between what they'd admitted in that kiss and the hushed darkness of his bedroom?

He kept a suite in the same Fifth Avenue hotel he'd stayed at when he'd first come east months before.

"You need this place for business, huh?" Cullen had said, when they'd met one evening for dinner.

Keir had put on his most innocent look. "Hey, why else would I want a view of Central Park from the bedroom?"

"From the bed, you mean."

"Yeah, well, that too."

"Oh, absolutely," Cullen had said, straight-faced, and then they'd grinned at each other and gone on to talk about other things.

Keir shot another quick look at Cassie.

Even Briana had teased him about what she'd dubbed his love nest, when she'd been in town a couple of weeks ago.

He'd evened the score by asking her how come a kid sister knew such things and Bree had sighed dramatically.

"Go right on living in a different century, BB," she'd said, "whatever makes you happy."

Keir frowned.

What was he doing? Thinking about his kid sister's sex life was the last thing he wanted to do. He didn't want to think about anybody's sex life, except his own. So why was he wasting time driving home, when he could have had Cassie in bed by now?

Keir stepped a little harder on the gas.

He wanted Cassie more than he'd ever wanted a woman, and the hotel was perfect for a romantic rendezvous. Not that he'd ever had one there. Too busy, he'd told himself, too tired at the end of each long week…but not tired enough to stop having X-rated dreams starring Cassie.

But he didn't want a perfect setting if it meant making love to her this first time in a room filled with the ghosts of transient strangers. He wanted to carry her into the dark silence of a room that belonged only to him, to a bed that belonged only to him…

A bed where he had slept alone, all these months.

Was that logical? Keir almost laughed. The hell with logic. He'd abandoned logic the day he hired Cassie. Tonight was just the inevitable result of that loss of reason. Right now, he felt like pulling into the clearing he knew was just ahead and taking her in his arms.

Tires squealing in protest, he swung the wheel hard, stopped under the sheltering canopy of the trees and shut off the engine. Cassie turned toward him, her eyes wide, her mouth trembling, and he silently cursed himself for being an ass.

The look on her face said she regretted what had happened. While he'd been wondering if he could wait until they reached home, she'd been reliving those moments at Lola's, when he'd shown all the subtlety of a caveman.

The passion ripping through him gave way to the need

to take her in his arms and comfort her. He undid his seat belt but she shook her head when he reached for her.

"Don't." Her voice shook. "What happened was—it was a mistake. Let's just—just put it aside and pretend it never—"

He kissed her, his mouth gentle against hers, his hands cupping her face. After what seemed an eternity, she sighed and he felt her lips soften. He kissed her one last time, then took her in his arms and held her close.

"I'm sorry," he said softly. "I shouldn't have come on to you like that, but—"

"You don't have to explain. Like I just said, it was a mis—"

He kissed her again, over and over until she was clinging to him, her heart racing wildly against his.

"The mistake was lying to each other—to ourselves—for so long," he said gruffly. "I want to make love with you, Cassie. You want the same thing." He felt a shudder go through her and he drew back and tilted her face to his. "If I'm wrong, tell me so now."

Cassie looked at him. That was what she'd intended to do, just before he'd pulled off the road. Tell him he was wrong, that this was wrong...

How could it be?

She'd never felt so alive in her life. The feel of Keir's hands on her. The taste of him. Even the sound of his voice...

"Cassie." He leaned his forehead against hers. "If you don't want me, say so. Because in a couple of seconds..." He made a sound that was half laugh, half groan. "In a couple of seconds, sweetheart, I don't think I'll be able to stop."

Cassie drew a shuddering breath. How could he do that? Turn her on with an admission of how much he wanted her, then touch her heart with a simple endearment that made her want to weep?

Foolish, she thought, oh so foolish. Men used words like

sweetheart all the time. They told women they had to have them, all the time. And what they said, in the dark heat of the night, was never what they meant, in the cool light of morning.

She knew all that, knew it, knew it…

And wanted him despite what she knew would happen later, the pain, the rejection, the cold light of morning's reality.

A cry burst from her throat. She clasped Keir's face, brought his mouth to hers and kissed him with all the pent-up hunger in her soul.

It was like touching a match to kindling. He said something quick and urgent, unsnapped her seat belt, pulled her across his lap, and when she gave another of those little cries he slid his hand under her skirt, feeling the heat of her skin, the coolness of lace and silk and then, yes, oh yes, the heat of her against his cupped palm.

She was wet and hot, writhing against his hand, moaning into his mouth, and it was all for him.

Now, he thought fiercely. Now, right here. Just tear off this bit of silk, free himself, bring her down and down and down onto his rigid, aching flesh…

Keir shuddered and drew back his hand.

Doing it took all the willpower he possessed. Cassie whimpered in protest, which was almost enough to make him act out the wild fantasy that had just flashed through his head, but he dragged in a deep, deep breath and clasped her shoulders.

"No," he said in a low voice. "Not here. I want to make love to you where I can see you. Where I can watch your eyes fill with me, see you tremble just before I take you over the edge."

Slowly, he took her arms from around his neck and eased her back in her seat. One last, quick kiss. Then he fastened their seat belts and took hold of the steering wheel with hands that were none too steady.

"Twenty minutes," he said hoarsely. "Then we'll be home."

Cassie nodded. She didn't trust herself to answer. Her heart was trying to leap from her chest; he wanted to see her tremble, he'd said, but she was doing that already.

Heat swept into her face. Keir was the one who'd stopped, not she. She'd been ready to let him take her here, in the car, just a couple of yards from a public road.

She'd never done anything like this in her life.

Women talked about spontaneous sex, especially backstage, killing time between numbers. Cassie hadn't. She'd listened, she'd laughed...but she'd never talked.

The other girls had joked about it.

"Cassie the virgin," they'd called her.

Well, she certainly wasn't a virgin. She'd fallen in love the year she landed her first job as a showgirl. Thought she'd fallen in love, anyway, which only proved how young and stupid she'd been. She'd tried to make the marriage work, but her husband hadn't understood either fidelity or love.

And there'd been men, after her divorce. Not many, but some. She was normal, she was healthy, she'd felt desire...

But never like this.

The hot, desperate need. The loss of control. The realization that nothing, *nothing,* was more important than the next kiss.

Better not to think about that. Better not to think about how this would surely end, because it *would* end, she knew that, and when it did...

"Leave it."

Keir's voice was rough. Her eyes shot to his face.

"Your skirt," he said. "Leave it the way it is."

She looked down. Her skirt was rucked at the tops of her thighs; she'd just started to tug it into place.

"Leave it? But—but..."

He reached across the console and touched her. The heart

of her. Just once, that was all, a caress as light as a whisper, but the stroke of his hand almost shattered her.

Cassie, who had never climaxed in her life, closed her eyes and knew she was lost.

The house was dark, looming against the moonlit sky like a medieval castle.

Keir got out of the car. By the time he came around to Cassie's side, she'd started to step out.

"Let me," he said softly, and gathered her into his arms.

She began to protest but he kissed her into silence and she sighed and buried her face against his throat.

She'd never been carried to a man's bed before...

And she had to stop doing this, thinking about what had been and measuring it against what was happening now. This night might be magic but, in the end, magic was smoke and mirrors.

Life had taught her that, more times than she wanted to remember.

Just commit this night to memory, she thought as Keir mounted the steps to his bedroom. All of it. The way Keir had kissed her when she was dancing with Carlos, branding her as his in front of everyone. The way he was holding her now, as if she was tiny and fragile when the truth was, she'd never been either.

"You're too big to be a dancer, Cassie," her mother used to say, but she didn't feel that way now, not in the strong arms of Keir O'Connell.

He shouldered open the door to his bedroom, whispered her name, kissed her mouth and then let her slip down his body to her feet. Her breath caught at his hardness, the taut muscles, all that beautiful masculinity so tightly leashed.

"Cass?" he whispered, and she understood. He was waiting for her to let him know that she hadn't changed her mind.

She lay her hands flat against his chest, raised herself to him and kissed him, openmouthed, telling him what she wanted, what she needed, and he responded instantly, angling his mouth over hers as he gathered her into his arms.

She felt the brush of his fingers opening the small buttons on her jacket, felt it slip from her shoulders to the floor. Heard the sibilant hiss of her skirt zipper. He fumbled with it just a little, and that pleased her, but he didn't try to ease the skirt down her hips.

"Wait," he said softly.

He lifted her hand to his mouth and kissed the palm. Then he went to the windows and opened the drapes, letting in the light from a sky radiant with stars.

He came back to her slowly, shrugging off his jacket and tie and dropping them on a chair. Her breath caught as he started to open his shirt. The way he looked at her, eyes dark and hungry as his gaze dropped to her breasts, outlined under the camisole, sent lightning arcing through her blood.

She thought of what she wore underneath. Better yet, what she wasn't wearing. No bra. No panty hose. A crimson garter belt, instead. A black silk thong. Sheer hose.

Why had she dressed like this? Was it for Keir? Had she known what would happen tonight?

Keir's eyes met hers. He said her name in a rasping whisper, but he didn't move.

My turn, she thought, and swallowed hard. She'd strolled the stage half-naked, danced while strangers gawked, stripped off her clothes as coolly as if she'd been alone. None of it meant a thing, not after the first few times. It was just a job. Bump, pay the rent. Grind, buy the groceries.

But tonight…tonight was different. She was going to undress for Keir. And—wasn't it silly?—she was nervous. Trembling, as if letting a man see her, naked, was something she'd never done before.

She licked her lips, forced a smile. Now, she told herself, and clasped the hem of the camisole…

Keir caught her by the wrists.

"No." His voice was still soft but it seared her like the desert wind. "Let me. I want to do it."

He wondered if the words had come out right. Cassie was looking at him as if he'd spoken gibberish. "Let me undress you, sweetheart," he said, and her lips curved in a smile that almost killed him with its sweetness.

One last taste of her mouth. Then he drew the camisole off.

She was braless.

She was braless and beautiful, adorned in red lace, black silk and ivory skin, and he was in danger of losing all his good intentions about going slow.

Cassie's hair spilled over her shoulders like black rain; her eyes were wide with wonder. Her breasts were perfect, just as he'd imagined them, round, high, the tips erect with desire. He spanned her waist with his hands and knew, when he saw those long, long legs, how they'd feel when they were wrapped around his waist.

If he didn't touch her soon, he was going to disgrace himself when he finally did.

"Beautiful," he whispered, and he lifted her into his arms and kissed her as he carried her to the bed.

Was it by some twist of fate that no woman had lain in this bed with him until tonight? Or was it possible, in some way he'd never understand, that he'd bought this bed for Cassie?

He covered her mouth with his, slipped his tongue between her teeth, tasted her sweet, warm essence. She moaned and he pressed his lips to her throat, felt the swift gallop of her pulse against his mouth.

How many men? The unwarranted thought brought with it a sudden, vicious pain, but her whisper drove everything else from his mind.

"Make love to me," she told him, just as she had in his dreams. "I want you so badly, Keir. I've always wanted you."

He caught her hands, kissed her palms, then rolled off the bed, stripped off the rest of his clothing and came back to her. He ran his hands down her leg, lifted her foot, slid it from her shoe, kissed the delicate, high arch, moved up her body and kissed her breasts, her nipples, until she was crying, pleading for his possession. He watched her eyes turn black as he slid his fingers under the thong, stroked the sweet, dew-wet flower that awaited him.

"Please," she said, "Keir, please."

With a low growl, he tore away the panties and entered her, driving hard, stunned at the heat, the tightness, the silken dampness all around him.

Too fast, he told himself, too fast, too fast, but it was too late. He tried to hold back, his muscles bunching with the effort, but Cassie arched toward him and he was undone. He groaned, moved, moved again, deeper, faster, faster until Cassie's sweet, sweet cry of release pierced the night.

Keir slid his hands under her bottom, lifted her, thrust deep one last time and then the wave engulfed him, stole his breath away, but instead of drawing him, spent, into a deep, bottomless sea it tossed him up to a place where the stars burned hotter than the sun.

"Cassie," he said, "oh God, Cassie…"

Her cry ran out again and this time he let go and fell over the edge of the world with her.

Sunlight. Hot light, pricking her closed eyelids.

Cassie gasped and shot up in bed.

The night came back in a rush, images blurred and spinning. How many times they'd made love. How wantonly she'd behaved.

How she'd climaxed, again and again, come with him inside her, with his mouth on her, his hands.

The first time. The very first time, and how right that it should have been with Keir. Only with Keir, she thought, and closed her eyes.

Dawn had been a soft promise on the horizon when they'd made love the last time. She'd started to rise from the bed but he'd drawn her back against him.

"Stay with me," he'd murmured. "I want to wake up with you in my arms."

But she wasn't in his arms. He wasn't even there. She was in his bed, alone.

Cassie sat up. One night. One incredible night, but that was all. Neither of them had pretended it would be anything more and she had no idea why she was fighting back tears. Keir hadn't lied to her. Wasn't that better than if he'd made a load of promises and—

"Hi."

She jerked the covers to her chin. Keir was standing in the bathroom doorway. His hair was wet; he had a towel draped around his hips and he was—her heart skipped a beat—he was gorgeous.

"I was just—" What? Leaving? Not naked. Not with her clothes scattered all over the room. How was she ever going to get them without putting herself on exhibit? She gave him a quick smile. "I was, um, I was just going to, uh, to—"

"Ah. Sure. Okay. There are extra towels, if you'd like to—"

"No. No, that's fine." Another smile. At this rate, she could try for a job selling toothpaste. "I don't have far to go. I'll, uh, I'll shower in my own place."

"Whatever you think best." He cleared his throat. "Well…"

Damn him! If he gave her another of those phony smiles, she'd stuff it down his gullet. He'd been awfully good at pretending last night. Couldn't he pull it off a little longer, make it seem as if he wasn't in a hurry to get rid of her?

"If you'd just…" She gestured toward the clothing strewn around the room. "If you'd just, you know, give me a few minutes…?"

He looked blank. Then his eyebrows shot toward his scalp.

"Oh. So you can get—"

"Yes."

"Sorry." He stepped into the bathroom. "Just, uh, just holler when you're—"

"I will." She waited until the door swung shut. Then she flew out of bed and began snatching up her things, blushing when she picked up the garter belt.

What in *hell* had she been thinking, wearing that?

No need to wear it. All she had to do was put on the suit. Just grab the other stuff, even her shoes, and get out of here before

"Dammit, Berk!"

Cassie whirled around as Keir stormed toward her, his expression as furious as his tone. She took a couple of quick steps back, clutching the clothes to her body. Her shoulders hit the door.

"Just what do you think you're doing?"

"I told you. I'm getting—"

"Dressed," he snarled. "And running for cover." He caught her by the shoulders and shook her. "The one thing I never figured you for was a coward."

Cassie's chin lifted. "You wait just a second, O'Connell. Who're you calling a coward? I'm not a—"

"The hell you're not."

Keir hauled her to her toes and crushed her mouth under his. She threw up her hands, shoved against his chest. It was like pushing against a stone wall. He thrust one hand into her hair, fingers hard against her scalp, forced her head back until she gasped and gave in to what she felt, what he was making her feel again.

Cassie wound her arms around Keir's neck and kissed him back.

After a long, long time, he took his mouth from hers.

"I don't want you to leave," he murmured. "Stay with me, Cass."

"I can't. It's no good. You know that. Last night was— it was wonderful, but—"

"Last night was only the beginning."

Cassie shook her head. She looked up at him, tears trickling down her face.

"I saw it in your eyes a little while ago. You knew—"

"What I know," he said, framing her face with his hands, "is that I'm not going to let you go."

"We're too different."

"Yeah." He grinned, ran his hands down her back and cupped her bottom. "I noticed."

"If we make love again—"

"And again, and again, and again." Gently, he wiped the tears from her eyes, then kissed them. "Look, you want the truth? I woke up, saw you lying in my arms and panicked."

"Exactly. Like I said, we're diff—"

"You work for me. That means I broke O'Connell's Rule Number One. Never get involved with someone who works with you."

Cassie gave a sad little laugh. "It's number one on my list, too." She hesitated. "And then there's—there's all the rest of it. You know, my—my background. It bothers you, doesn't it? That I—that I was a-a—"

"A showgirl. A cocktail waitress."

"A stripper." She felt him flinch, and she took a deep breath. "See? I'm right. It does—"

Keir swept her into his arms. "I'm no candidate for sainthood, sweetheart. And all I really know is that it feels right, to hold you. To make love to you." He paused, and she could see that familiar little tic in his jaw. "To wake up with your head on my shoulder in the morning." He gave her a slow, tender kiss. "Something's happening here," he said gruffly, "and I'll be damned if I'm going to walk away without knowing what it is."

He waited, his eyes searching hers, and, at last, Cassie cupped the back of his head and brought his mouth down to hers.

He carried her to his bed, came down beside her, and as

he lowered his head to her breasts, she knew that he was right.

Something *was* happening here. Something terrifying and dangerous.

She'd fallen head over heels in love with Keir O'Connell.

CHAPTER TEN

CASSIE lay sprawled over Keir, her head on his chest, one leg draped over his. His breathing was deep and regular. He was asleep but she…she was too filled with joy to sleep.

An unexpected snowfall had overtaken the sunny morning. Fat, lacy flakes of snow fell from a sky the color of fine old pewter.

What a perfect way to greet the day, Cassie thought dreamily. She loved snow. She'd missed it, all those years she'd lived in Las Vegas. It was the only thing she *had* missed about Denver.

Keir shifted his weight and murmured something in his sleep. Maybe his arm was cramped, from holding her. Her husband had never liked her to sleep so close.

C'mon, babe, he'd say after they had sex, *gimme some room, okay?*

She started to ease away. Keir, still sleeping, frowned and drew her even closer. Cassie sighed and buried her face against his chest. Such a simple thing, what he'd just done, and wasn't it silly that it made a lump rise in her throat?

There was no comparison between Keir O'Connell and her ex. She'd known that from the first minute she'd seen Keir, years ago at the Desert Song. He was everything her husband had never been, everything she'd never been.

Keir was educated. He was sophisticated. He'd traveled and seen the world; he knew things that never mattered until you realized you didn't know how to do them, like which fork to pick up when there were three to the left of your plate instead of one.

Most of all, he'd been raised in the warm bosom of a loving family.

She'd been raised by a mother who sometimes forgot Cassie existed.

Days like this, when she was a little girl, she'd snuggled deep into the blankets, tented them around her face so that all she could see was a narrow strip of the fire escape window behind the sagging living room sofa that was her bed.

On dark nights, especially when her mother hadn't come home, Cassie would lie on the sofa shaking with fear, eyes shut tight against the bogeyman she was sure would someday pop up and grin at her through the glass.

But oh, those snowy mornings.

Cassie smiled, shut her eyes and snuggled closer in Keir's warm embrace.

Safe under the blankets, her breath pluming into the cold air of the tiny apartment, she'd imagine mountains higher than the Rockies, where castles rose into the sky. She'd imagine what it would be like to live in one of them and take walks among the clouds.

She'd lie there until the last possible minute, just before her alarm went off.

Actually, it never really went off. She was always awake before then because her mother had threatened to throw the alarm clock out the window. It was, she said, too damned noisy, and how was a body supposed to get any sleep with it blasting her ears open all the way into the next room?

Cassie had only used the clock for security. She'd never missed school, not a single day. It was warm there, and safe, and the hot, filling soup in the lunchroom that most of the kids got free, same as she did, was the only meal she could count on.

And the after-school dance program, where she could pretend to be Odette in Swan Lake, or the Sugar Plum Fairy in The Nutcracker, if only for a little while…

For heaven's sake! What was the matter with her? That minutes-old lump in the throat was threatening to turn into a rush of hot tears. What was she doing, anyway, lying around like this? Stay with me, Keir had whispered, and

she had, and they'd made love again, and now it was time
to go.

Even if he'd meant what he'd said, that he wanted to go
on seeing her, she had her space. He had his. The best way
to keep the relationship going would be to honor those
spaces.

Carefully, she eased free of Keir's embrace. He muttered
a protest and she held her breath, waiting, but after a couple
of seconds, she could tell that he was still sleeping.

Her clothing lay in a little heap and she collected it as
quickly as she could, every now and then casting looks at
the bed to make sure Keir hadn't awakened. She blushed
again at the sight of the garter belt, snatched it up along
with the thong panties, went into the adjoining bathroom
and quietly turned the lock.

Looking in the mirror was a mistake but she did it anyway. Her hair was a tangled mess, her makeup was gone
and there were faint marks on her throat, her breasts...

Marks Keir had made, of his possession. Of the way he'd
made love to her, taking her up and up until she'd thought
she'd die of pleasure, then holding her in his arms as she
trembled in the aftermath of what they'd shared.

"Cassie," he'd whispered, that last time, "Cassie, you
don't know what you do to me."

She knew what *he* did to *her*, and if that was anything
like what she did to him, then she understood. If he'd felt
half as much of what she'd felt, she understood what he
meant. She hadn't told him that because words wouldn't be
adequate and besides, how much did she want to reveal?
Yes, she'd come—and come and come and come—for the
first time in her life, but it was more than that. Sex had
never made her want to weep with happiness, never made
her want to stay in a man's arms forever—

"Cassie?"

She swung toward the closed door, clothes clutched to
her breasts like a shield.

Keir's early-morning husky voice sent shivers down her spine.

Carefully, quietly, she cleared her throat.

"I'll be out in a minute," she called, and hoped she sounded casual and sophisticated, the way you were supposed to sound after you left a man's bed.

"Cass." His voice lowered; she could picture him leaning close to the door. "You know what I was thinking?"

Cassie dumped her clothes on the vanity, stared at the little pile of stuff, thought about how long it would take to get it all on and grabbed for her panties.

"What?"

"A long, hot shower would be terrific."

"You're right." One foot into the panties, then the other. Careful! She'd almost tripped. Wouldn't she be a lovely sight, lying in a tangled heap on the tile? Skip the stockings. The belt. Just the camisole. Good. Now the suit.

"Cassie? Did you hear me?"

Cassie zipped her skirt, slipped on the jacket, ran her hands through her hair. She looked as if she'd been doing exactly what she had been doing all night.

She'd made it a point never to let a man see her like this. A guy who dated a showgirl expected her to look like one. Her ex had pointed that out first, the morning after they'd taken their vows at the Las Vegas Starlight Chapel.

Glorying in the special pleasure of being married, in the intimacy of it, she'd showered, then come out of the bathroom in baggy sweats, her face scrubbed clean, her hair towel dried instead of carefully styled with a brush and a dryer.

Hank had looked up from the deck of cards he was fanning and done a classic double take.

"Jeez, babe you look like something the cat dragged in. Take the time you need, get yourself lookin' like my sexy lady and meet me downstairs. We'll get some breakfast at that buffet place on the Strip, okay?"

If there was only a buffet place around now. Anything

to distract Keir from taking a good look at her when she stepped out of the bathroom.

"Cassie?" Keir rattled the door knob. "Are you all right? Open the door. Dammit, Cassie…"

She turned the lock, swung the door open, smiled brilliantly at the stubble-jawed, hair-in-his-eyes, half-naked, beautiful man waiting for her with a scowl on his face.

"Hi," she said briskly. "Sorry I took so long, but—"

Keir cut off her words by hauling her into his arms for a kiss.

"Good morning," he finally said, against her mouth, "and what in heck are you doing in that get-up?"

She put a hand against his chest and stepped back a little, wishing the room might be plunged into darkness.

"I know. I'm a mess. My hair. My makeup. And this suit is all wrinkles. Well, that's the thing about silk. Looks great until you put it on, and—"

Keir put his index finger against her lips. "You're babbling," he said softly.

Cassie flushed. "Sorry. I just—"

"Caffeine."

"Huh?"

"You need caffeine." His arms went around her; he gathered her against him and smiled down into her eyes. "Come to think of it, we both do. Plus food. Eggs. Bacon. Sausages. Or bagels. You like bagels? The kind you can only get on the East coast? I admit, they're not New York bagels, but—"

"Keir. I have to, uh, to freshen up. You know. Take a shower."

"Uh huh."

"Do something with my hair. My makeup. My clothes…"

"The shower idea is cool. I mean, it was my idea in the first place, remember?" Smiling, he linked his hands at the base of her spine. "As for the rest of it—"

"Oh, I know." She flushed. "I'm a mess."

"A mess? Cassie, you're gorgeous." His voice softened. His eyes dropped to her mouth, then lifted to her face. "Your lipstick's all gone."

"Right. Well, give me an hour and—"

"I probably kissed it off."

"Yes. I'll fix it."

"Fix it? What for?" Gently, tenderly, he brushed his lips over hers. "I like your mouth just the way it is, sweetheart."

Cassie blinked. "You do?"

"Soft and sweet, just like you." Keir smiled. "You're beautiful. Have I told you that lately?"

She felt herself relaxing, leaning back against his linked hands.

"Not for the past hour, at least."

"In that case, I have a lot of making up to do. First, though, that shower. Then, breakfast. I know a diner ten minutes from here. Not fancy but the food's great. Did you ever have smoked salmon on your bagels? They call it lox here, on the wild and woolly East coast." He smiled at the look on her face. "Don't tell me. You're into yogurt and granola, right?"

Cassie smiled. "Yogurt and fruit."

"Whatever you want, sweetheart." Keir kissed the tip of her nose. "Okay. Enough playing around while my stomach complains that it's never been this empty before. Shower time, m'lady. Right now."

She nodded and started to step back. Keir frowned.

"Where're you going?"

"Downstairs. To my apartment. To shower."

"No way. You're showering here, with me."

"But I thought—I mean, I assumed—"

"You want to take our shower in your place? That's fine, if you insist." He waggled his eyebrows. "But I'll bet my shower's bigger than yours."

Cassie laughed. "Maybe."

"And I'll bet my water's hotter than yours."

"Just like a man. You think everything you have is—"

She shrieked as he lifted her in his arms, stepped into the shower with her and turned on the water. Laughing, he kissed her. She kissed him back. And they didn't get out of the shower until the water began to run cool.

Afterward, he dried her with a big, soft towel, wrapped her in his heavy terry-cloth robe, sat her in a wing chair in his bedroom while he dressed in faded jeans, an Irish fisherman's sweater and hiking boots.

Watching him was a joy. He was so masculine, so handsome, so at ease in his own body. How would it be, Cassie wondered, to watch him get dressed every morning, watch him get undressed every night? It would never happen; she knew that.

But it was easy, painfully easy, to dream.

Then he carried her downstairs.

"It's too cold to walk around barefoot," he said, when she protested. "Besides, the sight of you in those killer red shoes might be more than I can take without some food in my belly."

She laughed and lay her head on his shoulder. Her protest had been halfhearted, at best. She loved being in his arms.

"Your turn," he said, depositing her on her feet in her bedroom.

She didn't move.

He didn't seem to notice.

Instead, he began strolling around, looking at the pictures she'd hung on the walls, touching the little mementoes she'd placed on the dresser.

After a while, she took jeans and a pair of boots from the closet, a sweater, underwear and heavy socks from the drawers. She waited.

She couldn't bring herself to shuck his robe.

"Keir?" she said, in a small voice.

He turned and looked at her questioningly. She gave him a quick smile and held up the clothes she'd gathered and he said oh, sure, he'd be in the living room.

Cassie knew it really didn't make sense. She'd been almost painfully modest when she first started dancing professionally but really, how modest could you be when you were racing off stage to make a change in just a couple of minutes? There were always other people around. Men, not just women. Male dancers. Stage managers and gaffers and the lighting crew. You'd be pulling off your costume as you came off-stage and it didn't mean a thing.

This was different. This was Keir. He wasn't a guy who'd just bought a ten dollar beer for the privilege of watching her strut her stuff; he wasn't someone who'd taken her out a few times so he could show her off.

She couldn't be casual about her nudity in front of him.

She dressed quickly, started to put on her usual makeup and paused. Had he meant it when he said he liked her just as she was?

Time to find out, Cassie thought. She opened the bedroom door, went into the living room…straight into Keir's waiting arms.

"I was coming to get you," he said gruffly.

"Did I take that long?"

"No. Yes." He kissed her, hard, his mouth crushing hers, his fingers knotted in her hair as he tilted her head back. "Let's get out of here," he whispered, "before I forget why we decided to get out of bed and put on all these damned clothes in the first place."

She liked the diner, just as he'd figured.

He could tell.

"Yogurt and fruit is all I want," she'd said, when he gave the waitress their order.

"Sure. With a little of everything else on the side."

Cassie had sighed. "We'll never eat it all."

He'd thought she was probably right. Their booth was made to seat four but when the girl piled all the stuff he'd ordered on the table, there was hardly room left for the salt and pepper shakers.

But he was starved. So, it turned out, was Cassie. She ate her yogurt, polished off her eggs, a waffle, a pancake and some sausage and when he layered half a warm bagel with cream cheese, added a strip of smoked salmon and offered it to her, she hesitated, chewed on her lip—did she know what it did to him, to watch her do that?—and said, well, okay, she'd take a bite or two...

She finished it all. No apologies for her appetite. He liked that in a woman. He was tired of taking women to dinner, watching them nibble on this, nibble on that, decline dessert even as they looked at the pastry tray with hungry eyes.

Cassie ate like a real woman. She had a body like a real woman. In all his life, he'd never dated a woman like her, so free of artifice, so honest, so lushly beautiful. He'd joked about that mystical creature called the perfect woman with Sean and Cullen but until now, he'd never thought—never thought...

He sat back, shocked by where his thoughts were taking him. Nothing in this life was perfect and besides, what did that have to do with anything? A woman didn't have to be perfect to warm your bed and share some laughs...

"...burst!"

Keir cleared his throat. "Sorry. What did you say?"

Cassie groaned. "I said, I cannot believe I ate all that. One more mouthful and I'll burst."

He smiled, tried to get back to where he'd been just a few minutes ago, sort of floating in that nice comfort zone that came after a night of incredible sex.

Incredible? Hell, it had been more than that. More than sex. Well, no. What could that mean, "more than sex"? Sex was sex, and he'd had great times before...

But not like this.

How about Cassie? Had it been the same for her, or had she cried out in the dark for other men as she had for him? Had she made those little sounds that drove him wild for other men, as she had for him?

Had she? God, had she?

"Keir?"

He looked up, fought to focus on her face. "Yeah. Sorry. I was, uh, I was thinking about—about an order I took the other day, from, um, from The Pink Elephant. It's a new restaurant in the Village."

"Ah," Cassie said, as if she cared. As if it mattered to either of them how many cases of wine The Pink Elephant had ordered.

She asked questions about the restaurant and the wines they'd ordered. Intelligent questions, knowledgeable questions, or so his frazzled brain told him, even as he wondered why in hell he was talking about business when what he wanted to talk about was what had happened last night? It really couldn't happen again, even though he'd spent an hour this morning telling her that it could, because the truth was, she was right.

This couldn't work.

They were oil and water. They didn't have a thing in common, except in bed. She was his employee. He was breaking all his own rules and anyway, it was over. The sex. He'd gotten it out of his system.

How many other men had felt the same hunger for Cassie?

"Is that your name?" he blurted.

"What?"

"Cassie. Is it your real name?"

"Yes," she said slowly, "it is. Well, my given name is Cassandra, but—"

"I thought maybe you took it when you started dancing."

She sat back a little. Her smile tilted. He could almost feel the barricades going up. Why? All he'd asked was a simple question.

"As I said, my name is Cassandra. But nobody ever called me that. I was always 'Cassie.'"

"Oh." He nodded, picked up his coffee cup and stared into it as if he could read the ancient mysteries in its depths.

"Did you want to know anything else?"

Her tone was pleasant but something in it chilled him. Why was she upset? He had the right to ask her about her name, didn't he?

"No. Not really." He put down his cup, signaled to the waitress for refills. "So, what were you saying about *cabernet franc* grapes?"

She hesitated. He could almost see her trying to figure out what was going on. He was asking questions, was what was going on. What was so unusual about that?

"Well, I took a course. In New York. About viticulture, and one of the things I read about climates like this one—"

"I've always wondered. How does a woman get started, dancing in Vegas?"

She looked at him through eyes gone cold but it was only a question. He was just making conversation, was all. Why would it bother her?

"Are you asking in general, or are you asking me?"

"In general," he said, and shot her a fast smile.

"Amazing," she said softly, "that you managed the Desert Song for all those years and never got around to asking that question of any other dancer."

He'd asked. He knew all the stories. They ranged from having wanted to be the next prima ballerina to wanting to find a sheikh with a billion oil wells. Every showgirl he knew had her head so stuffed with dreams that there wasn't room left for a thimbleful of reason. Why would Cassie be different?

"You, then," he said. "How'd you come to be a Vegas showgirl?"

"Me." Cassie nodded. "Well, I decided I wasn't good enough for the American Ballet Theater."

"You studied ballet."

"And tap and modern dance." Her eyes narrowed. "My first love was ballet but after ten years of standing on my bloodied toes I decided, what the heck, Vegas would be more fun.''

Was it a joke? Her expression gave nothing away. Keir decided the safest thing was just to nod and look thoughtful.

"Makes sense."

"No, it doesn't." Her voice was low pitched, each word crisp and clear. "Nobody decides Vegas would be more fun. Not me, anyway."

"I understand."

"The hell you do!" Cassie leaned across the table. Her words were hard and rushed. "Growing up, I'd loved one thing, lived for one thing. Ballet. But there wasn't much of a market for ballerinas in my world."

Keir winced. "Cassie—"

"Reality was, I was seventeen and my mother was a drunk, and she had a new boyfriend who gave me funny looks. So I ran away from home."

"Cass." He reached for her hand but she yanked it back.

"We weren't all born with silver spoons in our mouths. Can you even imagine what it's like, trying to put a roof over your head when you haven't got a diploma or a skill? I waited tables in a zillion greasy spoons."

"Cassie. Please. I'm sorry. I only wondered...I mean, you seem so different...I mean..."

"You mean," she said coldly, "I didn't embarrass you just now by wiping my mouth on my sleeve, or by clutching my knife in my hand while I ate my eggs."

She tossed her napkin on the table, the rage bubbling inside her like lava in a volcano about to blow and the worst of it was, she had no right to be so angry. Oil and water. They'd never be able to mix, not if they tried for a thousand years.

"What's the matter, O'Connell? You having second thoughts about making it with somebody so obviously out of your class? Or is it the stripper part that's bothering you?"

"No," he shot back, and then his eyes turned black as

night. "Yeah. Okay. Maybe it is. Maybe I'm finding it tough to think about all the guys who saw everything that I saw last night."

She recoiled, just as if he'd physically struck her. He saw her mouth tremble and then she got to her feet and walked out of the diner.

Keir dug out his wallet, dropped bills on the table and went after her.

"Cassie!"

She was walking fast, heading along the road that led back to the vineyard. It was snowing harder than before, the temperature probably someplace around twenty degrees, and it was at least twenty miles to the house.

"Cassie, dammit!"

She walked even faster. He cursed, got in the Ferrari, gunned the engine and took off after her. When he pulled abreast of her, he put down the window.

"Get in the car."

"Keep away from me, O'Connell."

"Dammit, you want to freeze to death? Get in the car!"

"Find yourself a new manager. Someone new to play with, too. I'm moving out of that apartment tonight."

He pulled onto the shoulder of the road ahead of her, slammed on the brakes and jumped from the car.

"Damn you, Cassandra!"

Her name, her old-fashioned name that she'd always secretly thought sounded beautiful but had never used because beautiful names had no place where she'd grown up, was like music on his lips.

Cassie stopped. To her horror tears filled her eyes. She tried to walk around Keir but he matched her, step for step, and suddenly she was weeping and he was holding her so tight she could hardly draw breath.

"I'm crazy with jealousy," he said roughly, "and I don't know what to do because I've never felt like this before."

"That's because you've never been with anyone like

me," she said, sobbing into his jacket. "I told you, didn't I? We're not right for each—"

His mouth covered hers, stealing her words, her tears, her breath.

"It's because I've never cared for another woman the way I care for you. From the beginning, from that first minute I saw you that day at the wedding…" He framed her face, lifted it to his, thought his heart would break at the tears and snowflakes caught in her lashes. "I don't give a damn about anybody in your past, just as long as I'm the only one in your life now."

"Those legions of men, you mean?" Cassie gave a watery laugh. "I have an ex-husband. Aside from that, I've probably been with fewer men than—than most of the women you know. I don't—I don't get involved with men. They want only one thing and then, poof, they're gone."

"Not me," Keir said fiercely. "I want more. And I'm not going anywhere."

"I know you think so, but—"

"Listen to me, Cass. I'm not going anywhere. I just— I'm pleading with you to forgive me for what I said back there."

Cassie gave a hiccuping sigh. "It's okay."

"The hell it's okay! I should never… I'm not a prude, Cassandra. I don't have a thing about women being virgins while men are free to tomcat around. As for stripping…that was your choice, whatever the reasons, and who am I to second-guess them?"

Cassie smiled, wiped her nose on her sleeve and clasped his face between her hands.

"Here's my story, in a nutshell. No," she said, when he started to speak, "no, I want you to hear it. I left home at seventeen. I hitch-hiked from Denver, worked in diners, couldn't make enough to live on. When I landed in Vegas, the only job I could find meant doing the same thing. One day, a customer came in, looked at me and asked if I could dance. 'Could I dance?' I thought. Here it was. My big chance.''

She laughed in a way that made Keir's arms tighten around her.

"Aw, baby. Don't. Don't put yourself though this."

"I told you, I want you to know. See, I was so young, so dumb—"

"Innocent," Keir said softly. "That's what you were, sweetheart. Not dumb."

"I took his card, agreed to show up at the Casbah hotel." Her smile wobbled. "I auditioned. It wasn't ballet but I could do the routines. The costumes were beautiful. The pay was a zillion times what I was earning, so I took the job."

The snow was coming down in almost impenetrable sheets. Keir led Cassie to the car. They got in.

"Cass, that's enough. There's nothing wrong with dancing. I never thought there was."

"Do you know what dancing in those shows is like? Do you know that you have to audition for your job every six months?" She hesitated. "I had been dancing for a few years when, one night, I was running up the stairs to change my costume. I tripped, I fell…"

Keir gathered her into his arms and kissed her. "Sweetheart, please. No more."

"I blew out my knee," she said, sitting upright and looking into his eyes. "It took a long time to get better and I thought everything was fine but just before the next six month audition, the company manager called me aside. 'Cassie,' she said, 'I thought you'd rather hear this in private.' They weren't going to hire me for the next show. I couldn't get another job in any of the revues—they all knew about my injury. So I took a job stripping in a bar." Her voice broke. "That's what I am, Keir. A stripper. I always told myself I was a dancer but the truth—the truth—"

"Come here." Keir drew her against him, kissed her mouth, stroked her snow-dampened hair back from her face.

"You're one hell of a survivor, is what you are." He lifted her chin. "And the best damned manager I've ever had."

Cassie shook her head and buried her face against his shoulder. "Don't say things just to be kind."

"Me? Kind? Not when it comes to business."

There was a smile in his voice; it made her smile, too.

"You mean it? I'm good?"

"Yes," he said solemnly. "You are. You're innovative, you're tough but you're fair, you're great with people..."

"I was a lousy stripper."

She gave a forlorn little laugh. Keir, watching the quick play of emotion on her tear-stained face, felt as if his heart was expanding in his chest.

"You were, huh?"

"Oh, I was awful. The only way I could get through my turn was to tune out where I was and what I was doing. If you don't smile, don't wink, don't look as if you're having a good time, the tips are rotten. That's what you dance for, in a bar. The tips."

Keir tried not to let her see the rage building inside him. He wanted to beat the crap out of every jerk who'd been too stingy to tip this woman who'd had the courage to bare her body while never baring her heart. He took a couple of deep breaths, told himself to calm down, and worked up a smile.

"So you became a cocktail waitress instead, and wasn't that a fine thing to have done because otherwise, we'd never have met." His smile faded. "I'd never have found you, Cassandra."

He kissed her, his mouth moving softly over hers, and then he drew back a little and looked into her eyes.

"I'm not even going to comment on what you said about me having to find myself somebody else to play with," he said softly. "As for the rest... I don't need a new manager."

Cassie smiled. "I guess not."

"But you were right about the apartment. That you're going to move out, I mean."

Her smile wavered. "I don't understand."

"You *are* moving out. Tonight, sweetheart." Keir tilted her face to his. "And then you're moving in with me."

CHAPTER ELEVEN

SUNLIGHT poured into the kitchen of the manor house. The room was delightfully warm, thanks to the enormous brick fireplace that took up most of one wall; the handsome old stone floor was smooth and pleasantly cool under Cassie's bare feet.

She hummed softly to herself as she moved from the refrigerator to the oak table that stood in a cozy corner near one of the big windows, setting out glasses of orange juice, toasted scones and jam. The jam was from a farm just up the road; the scones were a special gift from the chef, who'd given them to her last night, wrapped in a pale blue linen napkin and still warm from the oven.

Living at Deer Run was lovely.

Living with Keir was the most wonderful thing that had ever happened to her.

It was hard to believe she'd never thought they had anything in common. They did. Loads of things, everything from shuddering at the sight of anchovies on pizza to midnight raids on the refrigerator to a passion for old jazz records.

She'd been right, that day she'd moved in to the apartment, he *had* been trying to sneak a look at her collection of 78's. He even had some early Ella Fitzgerald she'd searched for in every flea market within a hundred miles of Vegas, and she had a Miles Davis album he'd looked at like a kid on Christmas morning.

They both put the cap back on the toothpaste, loved English murder mysteries and hated old movies re-done in color. And if he thought today's boy rock groups were a joke while she thought, well, they were, but they were also awfully cute, she could forgive him because he was so wonderful, so incredibly wonderful, every other way.

Cassie turned off the coffee, filled a cup and added sugar and cream.

She was happy.

Happy. Such a simple word. Such a miraculous word. She was happy, for the very first time in her life.

She and Keir had been together only a little more than a month but it was already hard to imagine life without him...and that was something she tried not to dwell on because she was a pragmatist and she knew better than to think about the future.

They'd made no promises, though she would have, in a heartbeat, if only a miracle were to occur and he'd ask.

Sometimes, just every little once in a while, she let herself think that maybe he was falling in love with her. Could a man be so tender, so passionate, so attuned to a woman's every need unless he loved her?

Cassie's smile faded. Yes, of course he could.

That was the unadorned truth. The girls she'd worked with talked constantly about the men who said they loved them one moment only to toss them into the discard pile the next. Hadn't her ex done the very same thing to her, all those forever promises gone to hell in a handbasket?

How could a man kiss you off as if you were nothing? Hank had taken advantage of her so badly that by the time he walked out, she was glad to see him go.

She'd learned something, at least. She'd never let the guy be the one to do the walking, if she got involved again. *If*, because she'd vowed that she never would, not unless some miracle happened and The Perfect Man rode into her life.

Well, Keir was the Perfect Man. The trouble was, he didn't know it. He didn't know that she was his Perfect Woman, either, that she could make him happy, so very happy, if only—

"What does a guy have to do to get a cup of coffee around here?"

Cassie swung around as Keir came toward her. Seeing him made her heart fill with so much love that she felt as if it might burst.

"He has to learn to make the coffee himself," she said, smiling as he took her in his arms.

"I made it once," he said solemnly. "Remember?"

Their cooking arrangements were simple. Cassie did breakfast, Keir did dinner, but she always did coffee, once she'd tasted the wicked black ink he brewed.

Cassie rolled her eyes and looped her arms around his neck.

"Okay, I take it back. I'll do the coffee. You get out the butter and eggs."

"Yes, ma'am," he said, but instead of letting go of her, he gave her a long, tender kiss, then made a show of running the tip of his tongue over the softness of her bottom lip. "Umm. Coffee with two sugars and a dollop of cream. Just the way I like it."

"Sorry, pal. You'll have to pour a cup of your own."

"I've got a better idea. You take a sip of coffee..." His voice turned husky. "And I'll take a sip of you. How's that sound?"

"Like an eminently fair idea," Cassie said softly. She rose toward him and kissed him, teasing his lips apart, sighing with pleasure when he drew her closer...

"Dammit." Keir sighed, clasped her shoulders and put a couple of inches of space between them. "Baby, I'm sorry. I just remembered an appointment."

"Oh."

"In..." He glanced at his watch. "In just a couple of hours."

"Sure." Cassie stepped out of his arms. "I understand," she said, and she did. He had a vineyard to run. It was just that there were times, silly as it seemed, it hurt to be reminded that he was her employer, that that was their primary relationship. "Go on, sit down and have your breakfast. How do you want your eggs? Scrambled? Fried? Poached?''

"Sorry, sweetheart. No time."

"Oh," she said again. "Well—well, fine. I'll clean up here while you get dressed."

"No time for cleaning up, baby. Not if we're going to be in the city by noon."

She turned from the sink and looked at him. "We?"

"We. Definitely, we." Keir reached out and tugged her into his arms again. "You think I'm going to try and pick furniture for this place all by myself?"

"What?"

"Didn't I mention it?" he said, trying to sound casual in hopes she'd buy the story when the truth was, the idea had come to him days ago and terrified him so much he'd gotten tongue-tied, just trying to figure out a way to spit it out.

He'd never, in his entire life, wanted a woman to help him pick out anything, not even a tie.

Yes, the house needed furniture, stuff on the walls, drapes, blinds, all of that, and with winter here and things slowing down at the vineyard, he'd started to think about hiring a decorator. That was what he'd done when he lived in New York and again after he'd taken over the Song.

That had been his plan until last week when he'd awakened early one morning with Cassie's head on his shoulder and her hand on his heart and he'd thought, *Why would I want some stranger to put this place together when I'd much rather see this house through Cassie's eyes?*

A logical idea, after all, considering that they'd discovered they liked so many of the same things. There was just something about the ramifications that made it seem a—a step. A big step, though he was damned if knew toward what.

Cassie was staring at him as if he'd gone out of his mind. Maybe he had. Maybe he really had.

"You want us to choose furniture together?"

No. Hell, no. That wasn't what he'd said. Well, it was, but the way she said it made it seem so—so—

Keir cleared his throat. "Yeah. That's the general idea. I, ah, I made this appointment. With this, uh, this interior designer. I meant to tell you about it, but... I mean, I thought I had told you about it, but..." *Hell!* "Cassandra." He clasped her shoulders again, lifted her to her toes. "Come with me. Okay?"

"Okay," she said softly, and wasn't it ridiculous to have to blink back tears over such a simple request?

They drove to New York and met with the designer, who smiled at Cassie.

"Ah. Mrs. O'Connell. It's a pleasure to meet you."

Cassie turned pink. "I'm not Mrs. O'Connell."

Another "ah," and a glance at Cassie's bare ring finger. Keir narrowed his eyes and slid his arm around Cassie's waist. "This is Miss Berk. She's..."

What? What was she? How did you introduce the woman who was your lover? What did the etiquette books say on this subject, and how was it he'd never before been angry because the right word didn't seem to exist?

"Miss Berk works for me."

He felt Cassie stiffen and he couldn't blame her. Was that the best he could do?

"We're close friends."

Oh, God in heaven, had he really said that? Cassie jerked away from him and the designer uttered such a significant "ah" that Keir came close to hauling Cassie into his arms right that minute to tell her—to tell her...

"If you'll both follow me, please?" the designer said, and Keir took Cassie's elbow and dragged her with him through miles and miles of showrooms, where he finally got her to do something other than shoot him icy looks by pretending he was crazy for a tiger-print chair with carved paws instead of arms and feet.

"Don't be absurd," she said, and after that, his

Cassandra was back, saying exactly what she thought, snapping off his head when she thought it needed doing, facing down the haughty designer until the woman was reduced to saying, "Yes, Miss Berk, I couldn't agree more."

The afternoon that had started so badly ended with Keir the proud if confused owner of six figures worth of furniture and a promised delivery date of four months.

"Four months," he said to Cassie as they sat down for drinks at a table in a handsome old café in Greenwich Village. "Not too bad, I guess."

Cassie didn't answer. She was staring at her wine list and he picked it up and opened it, to see what she was looking at that was more important than he was. Nothing. That was what he could see, anyway. Nothing, because he knew he was in trouble again and, dammit, he had no idea why.

"Cass? You think that's about right? Four months?"

"It's perfect." Her smile was as phony as his. "It's a number you like, isn't it? First for my probation, now for furniture delivery."

Probation? Was she really concerned about that? Had the mention of a four month time period reminded her of it?

He smiled and took her hand. "You don't have to worry about probation, baby."

"Really."

"Of course. I thought you knew that. You've been off probation for a long time."

Cassie snatched back her hand. "I suppose it ended when I started sleeping with you."

Keir looked as if she'd slapped him. She wanted to bite off her tongue. What had made her say such a hateful thing? Oh God, she *knew* what it was, the awful realization that she had no real place in his life. She loved him and it was agony to go on pretending that she didn't.

He rose from the table. She did, too.

"Keir. Please. I'm sorry. I didn't mean—"

"Yeah," he said in a tone so cold it made her shudder. "Yeah, you sure as hell did."

"No! I swear—"

"Let's go."

He dumped some bills on the table and headed for the door. Cassie saw peoples' heads turn but she didn't care. What mattered was that she'd wounded him, and for the most selfish, stupid reasons.

What he'd told the designer was the truth.

She *wasn't* his wife; she *wasn't* his fiancée. She was just as he'd described her, his employee and his—his close friend, and whose fault was it if she couldn't come to terms with that? Keir had never, ever promised her anything more.

She ran after him, calling his name.

"Keir. Keir, please. I never thought—"

He opened the door to the Ferrari. "Get in."

Cassie hesitated, then did as he'd ordered. He slammed the door hard enough to make her jump, then stalked around to the other side and got behind the wheel.

"Keir. I know it wasn't like that. I—I'm sorry. I'm so sorry…"

"It doesn't matter."

"It does! Oh, Keir—"

He swung toward her, his eyes flat and filled with fury. "No apologies, Cassie. Hell, maybe it's time we were honest with each other."

"I wasn't being honest, I was being hateful." Tears glittered in her eyes. "I was hurt. Angry. I was—"

"What do you want from me?" he said, his words hot and sharp.

Her face drained of color. She stared at him blindly and then she began to weep as if her heart were breaking in two. Keir sat beside her, hands wrapped hard around the steering wheel, furious at himself, furious at her.

What *did* she want from him? Maybe the real question was, what did he want from her? He cursed, pulled her into his arms and kissed her until she was breathless.

"Your job hasn't a damned thing to do with what's happened between us," he said, his hands cupping her face.

"You want me to fire you so you can feel better about us being together? You want to quit working for me?" He kissed her again, his mouth hard and unforgiving on hers. "Tell me what you want, Cassandra, and I'll do it. Just don't play games with me, don't—"

Cassie grabbed his face, dragged his mouth to hers and kissed him.

"I want you," she said. "Only you."

He kissed her mouth, her hair, her eyes. She moaned his name and he knew that this time he'd never make it home. Instead, he drove to the hotel, took her to his suite, made love to her, with her, until exhaustion claimed them both.

They headed to Connecticut early in the morning, Keir clasping Cassie's hand in his over the gearshift knob. He didn't want to let go of her, not for a minute.

Something had happened last night, some bridge had been crossed. In that bedroom high above Central Park, Cassie burning in his arms like the heat of a thousand suns, he knew he'd found someone he'd been searching for all his life.

Her name was Cassandra Bercovic, a sad, neglected little girl who'd grown up to be a brave and beautiful woman.

How on earth had he ever been lucky enough to find her?

He'd held her in his arms in the soft afterglow of love-making and told her how he'd seen her as if for the very first time that night in Texas.

She'd sighed and said she'd never forget that night, the way he'd stunned her by stepping out of her dreams and into her arms.

"It was like a miracle," she'd said softly, "and when you stopped...when you made it clear you thought you'd made a mistake...I was hurt but in my heart, I understood. We come from such different worlds..."

He'd silenced the rush of words with a kiss, told her she had it all wrong, that he'd stopped making love to her that night because he'd realized he was moving too fast, but he knew she didn't fully believe him.

She *wanted* to, but she didn't.

He'd have to find a way to make her see that there were no differences between them.

Inside, where it mattered, they were the same.

He looked over at Cassie. She was asleep. He'd worn her out last night, made love to her over and over again, but it hadn't been enough.

He wanted more than that. He wanted to tell her...to tell her...

Keir swallowed dryly. Okay. This time, maybe he *was* moving too fast. He'd made so many changes in his life these last few months... It couldn't hurt to slow down. Plan things out. That was his specialty, wasn't it? Planning things calmly, logically, was always a good idea.

Deer Run lay silent and peaceful in the clear morning light. Keir parked in front of the house, stepped quietly from the car and gathered Cassie into his arms.

"Are we home?" she murmured.

Home. He smiled at the way she said it. "Yes, baby. We are."

She smelled sweet and warm as he carried her up the stairs and to his bedroom. *Their* bedroom. He told himself he was only going to undress her and put her to bed, but as he undid zippers and buttons and slipped her out of her clothes, she whispered his name. He looked into her eyes and felt his heart turn over.

"Cassandra," he murmured. "My Cassandra."

He carried her to the bed, his mouth never leaving hers, his kisses growing hungrier as hers grew more urgent.

She sighed his name, brushed her fingertips across his lips. "Keir," she whispered, "I've never felt—never felt—"

"What?" The word held all the urgency that had been building inside him. He swept her hair back from her face, cupped it, kissed her again. "Sweetheart. Cass. Tell me what you—"

"Oh, hell!" a voice said in gruff disbelief.

Cassie screamed. Keir swung around, fists raised, adrenaline surging through his body...

And saw his brothers, Sean and Cullen, standing in the open bedroom doorway, looking every bit as horrified as he felt.

CHAPTER TWELVE

THE three O'Connell brothers sat staring into the big stone fireplace in the living room.

Nobody spoke. Nobody moved. Nobody looked away from the flames dancing on the logs.

After a long, long time, Sean slapped his knees and got to his feet.

"Well," he said briskly, "this is an, uh, an interesting place you've got here, BB."

"Interesting," Cullen echoed. He nodded at a suit of armor in the corner. "I'll bet not many houses have a guy with a lance hanging around, just waiting for a joust."

"No," Sean said, "not many."

Sean and Cullen looked at Keir. Keir looked at them. Nobody could think of any more brilliant remarks so they went back to staring at the fire.

Time passed. Then Cullen cleared his throat.

"This room is enormous, you know? Has some nice features, though. All that molding, those great windows, the wide-planked floor..."

His voice trailed away. Sean leaped into the gap.

"Did you ever think about dumping all this old stuff? Buy a couple of pool tables, maybe a foosball table, too..." His brothers looked at him as if he'd lost his mind. "Hey, it's just a thought."

"Yeah." Keir rose and headed for the kitchen. "Anybody want another beer?"

"Great idea."

"Absolutely."

As soon as he was out of sight, Sean leaned toward Cullen. "What the hell's going on?" he whispered.

"Damned if I know," Cullen whispered back. "Only thing I *do* know is that our timing stinks."

"Man, does it ever. And, please, tell me I'm wrong, but wasn't that babe in bed with Keir the same one we saw in the elevator at the hotel?"

"I'd bet my last buck she's one and the same."

"Well, what's she doing here? Why hasn't Keir said anything about her except that she's too embarrassed to come down? I mean, I guess I can understand that, but how come he isn't talking about her? Your brothers trip over you playing games with a lady, you'd say something about the lady, wouldn't you?"

"Twice," Cullen said grimly. "We tripped over him twice."

"Exactly. So, how come he's not saying anything?"

"Like what?"

"Like what she's doing here, for starters."

Cullen nodded. "Yeah. You're right."

"I guess I'll just have to ask him."

"Let me."

"Why?"

Cullen frowned. "I'm older than you."

"What an intelligent answer."

"Look, let me handle it. I never mentioned it before because it didn't matter, but I know something... Ah!" Cullen sat up straight and shot a phony smile toward the arched doorway. "There you are, BB. Great. Another beer. Just what I wanted."

"Actually," Sean said, "I was kind of hoping to try some of your wi... No. Forget it. I guess this isn't a wine-drinking occasion."

Keir handed over the bottles and put one foot on the stone hearth.

"It sure as hell isn't."

"Look, man, if you want us to leave, you just say the word and we're out of here."

"Don't be foolish," Keir said, sounding more certain

than he felt. He shot a glance toward the stairs. Wasn't Cassie ever coming down? "It'll be fine. Just give her a little while."

Cullen nodded. "No problem. So, what were we talking about?"

"How to change this dungeon into a room," said Sean. "Remember? We were tossing around ideas, and you guys weren't clever enough to see that a couple of pool tables would do the job."

"A couple of dozen, you mean." Keir scowled at his beer bottle, raised it to his mouth and drank. "No need to do that. I already ordered furniture."

"Really," Sean said. Were they all crazy? There was a woman hiding in the bedroom upstairs, Keir was obviously upset, Cullen was hatching some kind of scheme and in the meantime, three healthy, heterosexual American males were talking about home decorating. "Let me guess. You ordered glass. Stainless steel. You know, like a doctor's office."

"Cherry."

"Huh?"

I went for cherry wood, plus some big, overstuffed arm chairs, a couple of sofas—"

"Leather?" Cullen said politely.

"Yellow and gray striped sailcloth for the chairs. Pale butterscotch suede, for the sofas."

Sean looked at Cullen. "Did the man really say 'striped sailcloth'?"

"Well, of course he did. It's a natural with the pale butterscotch suede." Cullen forced a laugh. "See what happens to a man when he moves east?"

Keir came closer to smiling than at any time in the past hour.

"*You* moved east."

"Yeah, but I didn't fall into the clutches of an interior decorator. Tell the truth. That's what happened to you, isn't it? You went someplace to buy a perfectly simple brown leather sofa and got brainwashed by a gang of decorators."

Keir sighed. "Well, I did spend yesterday with an interior designer."

"A designer, not a decorator," Sean said. He and Cullen moaned in unison. "That's even worse."

Keir actually managed a real smile. "Hey, it wasn't so bad."

"He wasn't wearing a velvet suit?"

"He wasn't a he."

"Yeah, well, that's no surprise."

"He wasn't a he because he was a woman," Keir said, and grinned. "And we really didn't take her advice all that much. We bought what we liked."

"We?" Sean said lazily.

"Yes." Keir took a breath. "Cassie and me."

Silence. Sean and Cullen exchanged a quick look. Then Cullen jerked his chin toward the ceiling. "Is Cassie the lady who…"

"Yes."

"Let me get this straight. You went shopping for furniture with that woman?"

"Her name is Cassie."

There was a warning tone in Keir's voice. Cullen heard it but ignored it.

"Correct me if I'm wrong here, BB, but wasn't the lady we're discussing the same one who was with you in the elevator the day Ma and Dan got married?"

Keir tilted the bottle to his mouth and drank the last of the beer.

"Yes."

"You brought her east with you?"

"No."

"Yes. No." Cullen gritted his teeth. "Is that all you can say?"

"I can add name, rank and serial number," Keir said coldly, "if it makes you feel better."

"What's that supposed to mean?"

"That I don't like being interrogated, and I don't like the tone in your voice."

"Well, that's too bad. How do you expect me to sound, huh? You, buying furniture with a babe you were screwing around with in—"

Keir grabbed Cullen by the front of his sweatshirt and hauled him to his feet.

"Watch your mouth!"

"Let go of me," Cullen said quietly.

"She's not a 'babe,' Cullen. You got that?"

"Let go, dammit!"

The men stared at each other. Then Keir lifted his hands carefully from his brother's shirt and stepped back.

"I'm sorry," he muttered. "I know you didn't mean... Hell, I don't know what's wrong with me. I guess what just happened, you guys suddenly turning up the way you did... It was kind of rough, not just for Cass but for me, too. I mean, looking around, seeing you there... I guess neither of you ever heard of a doorbell."

Cullen smoothed down his shirt, shot Sean a look. Sean was standing with his arms folded, his face blank, but Cullen was sure of what his brother was thinking. "Let me handle it," he'd told him, but so far he hadn't done much except tick Keir off.

"Yeah, well, we rang. We even banged on the door with that two ton chunk of brass you laughingly call a knocker. When nobody answered, we tried the door and found it open, came inside and then Sean said he thought he heard somebody upstairs."

"Terrific," Sean said, with a tight smile. "Blame it on me. The thing is, Cullen's right. We're sorry we walked in on you but how were we supposed to know that you... I mean, it's mid-morning, and..." He cleared his throat. "You can't blame us for wondering what's going on, BB. First we stumbled across you and this, uh, this woman—"

"Her name's Cassie," Cullen said, shooting Sean a "you're on dangerous ground, so take it easy" look.

"Right. Cassie. We saw you with her at the Song. It was nothing, you said. She was just a cocktail waitress, you said. Now—"

"I never told you she was *just* a cocktail waitress. What I told you was, she was a cocktail waitress."

"Isn't that the same thing?" Sean asked in an exasperated tone. He looked at Cullen, who'd gone back to pretending he was the Sphinx. "Okay. Never mind what she does."

"What she does is, she manages my restaurant."

"Here?" Sean said, blowing past caution and letting his voice reflect his surprise.

"Yes, here," Keir said coolly. "Where else would it be?"

"The lady manages—"

"Cassie. The *lady* has a name. Try and remember it."

"Take it easy, man," said Cullen. "We're just trying to put the pieces together. So, you brought Cassie with you from Las Vegas?"

Keir started to tell Cullen to mind his own business, thought better of it, and took a deep breath before he spoke.

"No. I didn't. I didn't even know she'd applied for this job."

"In other words," Sean said slowly, "she followed you to Connecticut?"

"No! Dammit, she had no idea I was... Look, forget the details, okay? The bottom line is that she came here, I hired her, and now..."

"And now," Cullen said carefully, "you're sleeping with her."

Keir swung toward him, the bones in his face showing sharp beneath his skin.

"Be careful what you say," he said softly.

"Well, it's the truth, isn't it?"

"Cullen. I'm warning you..."

"Yeah. I know you are, but why? Since when are we so circumspect about our sex lives?"

"Since Cassie." The muscle in Keir's jaw knotted and unknotted. "The topic's off limits. You got that?"

"How long have you known this woman?"

"What's the difference?"

"Just answer the question, okay? How long have you known her? How well?"

"It's back to interrogation time. Listen, Mr. Hot Shot Attorney, this is not a courtroom and I am not on the witness stand."

"Hey, you two, let's cool down, okay? Cullen is just curious. Aren't you, bro?" Cullen didn't answer and Sean rushed ahead. "Well, if Cassie worked at the Desert Song, then Keir probably knows her pretty well. Right, Keir?"

Keir's response was curt. "We'd never said much more than hello and goodbye until I stood up for Gray Baron at his wedding last summer."

"Oh." Sean nodded. "Well, no problem. That means you've known her for, what, five, six months?"

"Maybe you want to count the days and the hours, too." Keir's tone was ominous. His brothers meant well. He understood that, but there was something in the air, in Cullen's eyes, that he didn't much like. "Or maybe you'd like to check the lady's references."

"Keir," Sean said, "we're only looking out for you."

"Cullen?" Keir said, ignoring Sean, keeping his eyes locked to Cullen's, "how's that sound to you?"

"You want an honest answer?" Cullen folded his arms and rocked back on his heels. "I already checked them."

"You what?"

"That scene in the elevator piqued my curiosity. It was so uncharacteristic of you that I decided to find out a little something about Miss Cassie Berk."

"Who the hell do you think you are?" Keir's voice was frigid. "My life is my business."

"You're an easy mark, Keir. You always bleed for the underdog."

"Bleeding for the underdog, as you so graciously put it,

doesn't make me an easy mark, and what do you know about it, anyway?''

"I know what happened at the Song last year, with the girl your pal Gray ended up marrying, how she worked for you and you kept her on, even after you found out she'd falsified her references.''

"How do you know that?'' Keir demanded furiously. "That was private business.''

"The duchess told me.'' Cullen nodded at Sean. "She told both of us. She thought it was wonderful, how you'd done the right thing. Well, maybe it was. By ignoring the rules, you probably saved the girl's life.'' He paused. "Well, it's your life at stake now, pal.''

Keir, hot with fury, knotted his fists, and fought to keep his temper in check. Cullen meant well. He had to keep remembering that.

"Cullen.'' He spoke softly, biting off every word. "I appreciate your concern. I really do. Now, do us both a favor and get the hell out of my house before either you or I do something we'll both regret.''

"Your Cassie has guts, I have to give her that. Following you all the way here…''

"Shut up.''

"And she has a history.''

"I know her history.''

"She was a showgirl.''

"Get out, Cullen.''

"She was a stripper.''

"Out,'' Keir roared, pointing to the door. "You hear me? Get the hell—''

"What you've got, BB, is nothing but a bad case of ZTS.''

Keir threw a quick right at Cullen's jaw. Cullen parried it and came back with a left. Sean yelled, jumped between them and pushed them apart with an iron-hard hand on each chest.

"Are you two insane?'' he said, looking from one red,

angry face to the other. "Since when do the O'Connells fight over women?"

"Get this straight," Keir said, breathing hard, "I'm not going to let anybody, not even you, Cullen, say anything against Cassie."

"You're not, huh?"

"No!" Keir struggled against Sean's restraining hand. "And if you don't believe me—"

"Oh, I believe you," Cullen said. A wide smile curved his mouth. "By the way, that right of yours might be quick, my man, but it isn't much."

"The hell it isn't. You want to try it again... What are you laughing at?"

"Wasn't it usually you, peeling Sean and me apart, back in the old days?"

"That was just horsing around."

"Kidstuff. And I guess we've all grown up, huh?"

"I'm not much in the mood for a trip down memory lane."

"How about for a trip into the future, where you and Cassie Berk go down the aisle? That *is* what you have in mind, isn't it?"

"Damned right, it..." Keir realized what his brother had just said, what *he'd* just said, and stopped in the middle of his sentence. "What?"

"I admit, I checked up on your lady. And I'm not going to pretend I wasn't a little worried when I found out she had a, uh, a colorful past."

"She did what it took to get by," Keir said coldly, "and that's all she did—not that she needs your vote of approval."

"No. But she has it."

"Well, that's just too damned..." Keir blinked. "What'd you say?"

"Your lady has my approval. She'll do the O'Connells proud. Besides, you love her."

Keir look from one of his brothers to the other. Cullen was grinning, but Sean looked as bewildered as he felt.

"I didn't say—"

"Give me a break, Keir. You love her. And she loves you. Obviously, she told you all about herself, even though she must have gone through hell to do it. The lady loves you, man. Not your bank account, not your name. Just you."

"You've lost me," Sean said. "Cullen? What the hell are you saying?"

Cullen gave a dramatic sigh. "It's such a burden to be the only one in this trio with a brain. Look, it's simple. I figure that any female who can talk my big brother into wandering through a furniture showroom, who can make him so deaf he doesn't hear the doorbell ring, who can make him willing to take on his own flesh and blood to defend her honor, must be very special."

Nobody moved. Nobody spoke. Then Sean began to chuckle.

"Well," he said, "well, well, well." He dropped his hands to his sides and grinned at Cullen. "When you said, 'let me handle it,' I didn't know you were going to try for an Oscar."

"I played the scene by ear," Cullen said with modesty, "but I was pretty good, wasn't I?"

"Yeah," Keir grumbled, "and a lot that little gold statue would have meant, once I'd broken your jaw."

"You'd have been in the emergency room beside me, pal, lying right on the next table."

The O'Connells looked at each other, their faces solemn. Then Sean grinned, followed by Cullen and, at last, Keir.

"You idiot," Keir said fondly.

"Same to you, pal," Cullen said.

Keir punched Cullen in the arm. Cullen passed it along to Sean, who returned it to Keir. They grinned at each other again.

"Well," Keir said, "this calls for a bottle of Deer Run's best."

"After beer?" Sean made a face.

"You want to skip it?"

Sean smiled. "No way, man. I'll make the sacrifice."

Keir chose a merlot, opened it and poured three glasses.

"So," Cullen said, after the wine had been sniffed, tasted and admired, "you've finally fallen in love."

Keir felt himself blush, right down to his toes. *In love*, he thought, *me, in love.* "Yeah."

"So have I," Sean said, trying to look serious, "at least a dozen times, but I didn't see you guys getting excited about that."

Cullen sighed and put his hand on Sean's shoulder. "You don't get it, kid. This is L-O-V-E. The real thing." He smiled at Keir. "When do we get to meet the lady?"

It was a good question. How long did it take a woman to get over seeing two guys pop up in the doorway at the worst possible minute?

"Soon. In fact..." Keir put down his glass. "I'll go up and get her."

"Maybe you want to let her come down at her own pace. Or maybe we should leave, drive around a little, you know, then come back."

"No, don't be silly. Cassie has a terrific sense of humor," Keir said, mentally crossing his fingers and hoping he was right. "I'll give her a couple more minutes, then go up and talk to her. I'm sure she'll want to meet you two. She didn't meet you, not really, that last time."

"Does she know how you feel about her?" Cullen asked.

"You mean, have I come right out and told her that I love her?" Keir put another log on the fire. "No. The words are tough to get out, you know? Tougher still to accept inside yourself, where it counts." He swung toward Sean and Cullen, hands out in supplication. "But she knows. She has to know, right?"

Cullen eyed his brother over the rim of his glass. "It's

been my experience that women like to be told these things.''

"His experience," Sean said, and snorted. "Like, he knows about this stuff."

"They want to hear the words," Cullen said quietly. "Trust me on this, Keir. If you love her, you have to tell her."

Keir nodded. "You're right. I will. Hell, I want to." He smiled. "Then I'm going to take her home to meet Ma. I have the feeling they're going to get along just fine."

"Well, Ma knows Cassie, right? From the hotel? And from that wedding last summer?"

"Yeah, but this'll be different." Keir's smile tilted. "It's not every day you introduce your mother and the woman you intend to marry." He paused. "Cass will probably be nervous."

Sean grinned. "Who wouldn't be, meeting the duchess?"

"It's not that. Cassie has this thing about us coming from different worlds."

"Ah." Cullen poured himself more wine. "Prince Charming meets Cinderella. Not that you're a prince or in any way charming, mind you—"

"Thanks."

"You're welcome. Yeah, I can see how Cassie would be edgy but once you give her the chance to see the O'Connell clan in action, she'll stop figuring we're royalty in, what, ten seconds flat?"

Sean reached for the bottle of wine, refilled Keir's glass and his own.

"You know," he said slowly, "it just hit me... Ma's birthday is next month."

"So?"

"So, I spoke to Megan the other day, and she says Dan's planning a big party. You'll fly home for it, won't you?"

"Of course."

"Well, it's perfect. Bring Cassie with you."

Keir nodded. Perfect was the word. His mother, his sisters, his whole family would have the chance to get to know Cassie...

And the chance to overwhelm her.

A houseful of O'Connells was a lot for most people to handle. You needed a strong dose of stamina and lots of self-confidence to get through a first encounter.

Cassie—his Cassie, he thought with a smile—was tough and self-confident, but she still had that stubborn conviction that he and she came from different worlds.

Would she feel intimidated?

His mother would be warm, but she'd scrutinize Cassie's every move. His sisters would be welcoming, but they'd ask her a million well-meaning questions. And his brothers would bring her into the family fold with loving, if merciless, teasing.

It would be better to fly to Vegas when nobody was around except his mother and Dan. Next week. No. Why wait? This week. He could almost imagine how wonderful it was going to be to put his arm around Cassie and say, "Ma, this is Cassie. She's going to be my wife."

"Well?" Sean gave Keir a nudge in the ribs. "What do you think? You want to take your lady home to Vegas for the duchess's birthday party?"

Keir frowned. "No," he said slowly, "no, I don't."

Cullen nodded. "Maybe you're right. I mean, that whole scene...all of us, and then Cassie... It might be a setting for disaster."

"Exactly. That's the last place in the world I'd want to take Cassie. A big family party, the O'Connells all gathered around the table? Makes me shudder to think about it. Cassie would just—"

"Keir?"

"I mean, even if things went well, Cassie might simply—"

"Keir," Sean hissed, jerking his head.

Keir turned around. He saw Cassie, in the doorway. His Cassie, so beautiful, so alive, so...

Angry?

Oh, man. Not angry. Furious. Her green eyes were blazing like the flames of hell.

"Cass," he said, going toward her, "I'm so glad you decided to come down. I was just about to come upstairs and see if you were—"

Cassie slugged him. There was no other way to describe it. She hit him, hard, in the jaw. His head flew back; his ears rang with the force of the blow. For one awful moment, he saw bright white stars against a bright red background.

"Cass," he said, bewildered, "sweetheart..."

"You—you son of a bitch!"

"Baby—"

"You no good, arrogant, egotistical, self-centered bastard!"

She raised her hand again. Keir grabbed her wrists and locked both her hands against his chest.

"Honey, what is it? I know. You're still upset because these two jerks busted in on us, right? Well, they're sorry. Tell her you're sorry, guys. Cullen? Sean? Tell Cassie that—"

"Tell me what? That the whole miserable bunch of you are afraid I might use my salad fork for the roast beef?"

"Huh? Cass, baby—"

"Do *not* call me baby! Do not *ever* call me baby." Cassie wrenched her hands free and jabbed her index finger into the center of Keir's chest. "What else, O'Connell? What other things might I do to embarrass you at that fancy table? Forget to use my napkin? Eat my peas with a spoon? Slurp my soup?"

"Cassie, you accused me of this same kind of stuff before. And I told you—"

"You're right. I did. And you told me I was wrong. Okay. Let's cut to the chase, then. My very presence would embarrass you. It's one thing to tell a woman that you don't give a damn about her past, but that story falls flat when the past suddenly counts, when the possibility arises you might take that woman home to meet the folks instead of to your bed.''

"Cassie, for God's sake, you have it all wrong.''

"No. I have it right. I *always* had it right!''

"You know what, Berk? I don't know what in hell you're talking about.''

"That's the sad truth. You really, truly don't. You want to sleep with me, make me look like—like an idiot in front of your brothers—''

"What? Cass, that's crazy. I didn't know they were going to show up. I never—''

"You never. Well, I never, either.'' Cassie took a step back. "I categorically, absolutely, positively, never want to meet the rest of your horrible family. You got that?''

Keir looked at his brothers in bewilderment, but there was no help coming from them. Sean was studying his fingernails with meticulous interest; Cullen was showing the same concentration on the wine bottle label.

Okay, Keir told himself, Cassie was upset. It was up to him to calm her down.

"Sweetheart,'' he said, reaching out for her, "honey—''

"Don't call me that, either, dammit.'' Cassie batted his hands away. "And don't you *ever* kid yourself into thinking I'm angry because I give a damn for you, Keir O'Connell. I never did. You were just—just a man who offered me a good job and—and a good time for as long as it lasted.''

She spun away, ran for the door, grabbed her purse and her coat from the chair where she'd dropped them not two hours before. Two short hours before, when she'd been fool enough to imagine the man she loved was starting to fall in love with her.

So much for dreams, she thought bitterly, and slammed the door behind her.

CHAPTER THIRTEEN

KEIR stood frozen to the spot.

"What just happened?"

"Your lady's seriously angry," Sean said dryly, and cleared his throat, "that's what just happened."

Keir hadn't even realized he'd asked the question aloud until he heard Sean's response. He turned to him, arms outstretched.

"But why? Over what? What did I do, except say that I loved her?"

"Well," Cullen said with lawyerly caution, "as a matter of fact, you didn't. You told us but that was about it."

"Dammit, Cassie's the smartest woman I ever met. She must know..." Keir drew a deep breath. "Okay. You're right. I didn't tell her, and maybe she doesn't know, but I still don't get it. What in hell did I do to deserve all that?"

His brothers frowned, looked at each other, shrugged their shoulders and in general went through the puzzled motions of men agreeing they couldn't possibly comprehend the behavior of the exotic species known as the human female.

A car engine roared to life.

"She's leaving," Sean said.

"Probably going for a drive to cool off," said Cullen.

"She'd damn well better cool off," Keir said grimly. "Hell, here I was, telling her how much I adore her—"

"About to tell her," Sean pointed out. "Remember? You never actually—"

"What the hell's the difference?" Keir growled. He stalked across the room, turned on his heel and stalked back. "I'm in love with a woman for the first time in my

176

life and she calls me names. I'm an SOB, she says, an egotistical, self-centered…'' He stopped pacing, folded his arms and glared at his brothers. ''Don't bother telling me to go after her.''

''Well,'' Sean said cautiously, ''you want my opinion, BB, it might be a good idea if—''

''She'll be back soon enough.'' Keir shot a look at his watch. ''An hour, max. And when she gets here, she's going to have a lot of explaining to do.''

''Uh, you want us to leave? I mean, when she gets back you guys might want some privacy.''

''Nonsense.'' Keir strode to the door and grabbed his jacket from the chair. ''Let's go have lunch.''

''Great,'' Cullen said, so heartily that Sean winced. ''We've been dying to try your restaurant.''

''It's not open on Mondays. There's a diner. We'll go there.''

''Yeah,'' Sean said, ''but if Cassie should come back while we're gone…''

''How come you're busy telling me what Cassie will or won't do?''

''Listen, I know you're upset, but…it's just that there've been times I've felt kind of the way she might be feeling. You know, on the outside, looking in?''

''What the hell are you talking about?''

Sean thought about pointing out that he was the brother who wasn't the reliable one, who didn't have a law degree hanging on the wall… Damn. Keir was right. What the hell *was* he talking about?

''Nothing,'' he said with a quick smile. ''I guess I'm just taking a page from your book. You know, bleeding for the underdog.''

''Yeah, well, let's go eat,'' Keir said gruffly. ''Cassie gets back before we do, she'll wait.''

It wasn't until they were seated at a table in the diner, everybody looking at their hamburgers and nobody actually eating them, that he let himself wonder if she really would, or if his anger at her accusations—his pain at her inability to see into his heart and know that he loved her—had made him blind to the truth.

Maybe—just maybe, he should have gone after her.

By evening, he was positive of it. He'd gone to the door a hundred times, a thousand times, opened it and looked down the driveway hoping to see her car coming up the hill.

Sean and Cullen were gone. They'd wanted to stay, but he'd told them he'd be fine, that they were right and it was best if he was alone when Cassie came home.

The truth was that he couldn't look into their eyes without seeing they were thinking the same thing he was.

Maybe she wouldn't come back.

Maybe she'd left him for good.

Keir ran to the bedroom. Her clothes were all in the closet. Of course they were. He'd have seen a suitcase, had she taken one with her.

He thought of what she'd told him about how she'd left home when she was seventeen with little more than the clothes on her back and a toothbrush.

"It's not so hard to travel light," she'd answered when he said that must have been tough. "If you're running from something you're eager to leave behind, all that matters is getting away."

Keir sank down on the edge of the bed. One silk stocking lay draped across his pillow. He picked it up, felt its softness as it slipped through his fingers.

Was he one of those things Cassie could leave behind? He couldn't believe that. She loved him. He knew she did. He'd felt it in her kisses, heard it in the way she said his name for weeks now. Why hadn't he told her how he felt? Why had it taken him so long to figure it out?

And what had he done to send her running from him?

He rose to his feet, paced back and forth like a leopard in a cage, trying to figure out what had happened. He'd been talking with Sean and Cullen. About what? About taking Cassie home to meet the duchess.

Sean had suggested bringing her to meet the family for their mother's birthday. And he'd said no, that wouldn't work, that Cassie might be in over her head.

That was when she'd come flying at him like a tornado.

Keir ran his hands through his hair until it stood up in little peaks. Had he insulted her by suggesting meeting the O'Connells all at once might be too much? Maybe. Maybe not. Maybe...

"Oh hell," he said softly.

Everything he'd said, everything she'd have heard, was coming back to him like a tape recording. Him, saying how home was the last place in the world he'd ever want to take her. How all the O'Connells would be gathered around the table and how Cassie would be lost in their midst, except he'd never gotten all the words out, never said she'd be lost.

There was more. He'd told his brothers that the thought of her being there, of taking her home with him, made him shudder.

"Cassie," he whispered in despair, knowing how it must have sounded, knowing what she'd probably thought because it fed right into her refusal to see that they weren't different, that they were meant for each other, always had been meant for each other.

And he knew in that instant that she wasn't coming back. She was gone. Gone, and it was up to him to find her and make her know that he adored her...

That if she left him, he'd be empty, forever.

Keir ran downstairs, threw on his jacket, grabbed his keys and raced out the door.

Cassie had left the house on a rush of hot anger but by the time she'd gone half a mile she began to weep.

She pulled over to the side of the road, sobbed until her

eyes were bone dry and aching. Then she told herself to stop all this nonsense and make a plan.

One thing was certain. She was not going back to Keir's house. She didn't want to see him ever again, the bastard. The rat. The…

She wept again, until she was hiccuping. Then she dried her eyes, reminded herself that crying had never solved a problem in her life and forced herself not to think about anything but what to do.

She had her purse. Her credit cards. Her driver's license and her bank card.

The solution was simple. She'd go back to where all this had started. Las Vegas. She knew people there. She could get a job. She could move in with one of the girls she'd worked with, just until she was on her feet. She could arrange to have her things packed and shipped to her.

Where there was a will there was always a way.

The one thing she couldn't do was sit here much longer because Keir would be coming after her.

He would…wouldn't he?

She glanced in the rearview mirror, afraid to see the Ferrari barreling along the road…praying to see it.

No Ferrari. No Keir.

No dream. Not anymore.

Cassie wiped her eyes on her sleeve. Where next? Could she get a last-minute seat on a flight to Vegas? Probably. Lots of planes went there. It was a popular destination. At worst, she'd fly standby.

The only question was, which airport? Hartford, where she'd flown in? Providence, which she now knew was even closer? Boston, which was further away but might have more flights?

Providence, she decided, for no better reason than that "providence" was pretty much where she was putting her trust.

She put the car in gear and headed east.

Hours later she sat in the Trans-America waiting area at

T.F. Green Airport and watched, fingers crossed, as the two clerks behind the departure desk poked at their computer terminal keyboards, then held a quick conversation.

The nine o'clock flight to Las Vegas would be boarding soon. With luck, she'd be on it.

Two other flights had already left without her. She'd almost made it onto the one that had gone out two hours ago, but at the last minute a ticketed passenger had come rushing up, panting, boarding pass in hand, and Cassie had sighed with disappointment and gone back to her seat.

This flight looked pretty good. The clerks had been paging one passenger for the last fifteen minutes. If he didn't show soon she was home free.

Keir would never see her again. Keir, who hadn't cared enough to come after her. Keir, who'd used her the same way as her husband.

Tears pricked her eyes. Cassie blinked them back, folded her hands in her lap, and waited to hear her name called so she could board the plane that would carry her away from the last man she'd ever let use her again...

A man she'd loved with all her heart.

What a fool she'd been.

Keir skidded into a parking space at the airport in Providence.

She had to be here. Dammit, she *had* to.

He'd driven all the way to Hartford's Bradley Airport and checked every airline. All that day's flights to Vegas were gone and no matter what stories he'd concocted, he couldn't get anyone to confirm whether or not Cassie Berk had been on any of them.

Maybe she'd flown out of Logan, he'd thought, in Boston.

He'd gotten behind the wheel again, raced back the way he'd come. On impulse he'd gotten off the highway and stopped at the gas station on the main road that led to the vineyard.

The guy pumping gas listened to his description of Cassie and her car, scratched his whiskery jaw, chomped on a wad of tobacco a couple of times and finally said, yeah, a woman like that, in a car like that, had stopped for gas hours back.

"Asked how to get to Providence," he'd added, and Keir had hopped back into the Ferrari and roared away. On the way to the airport he'd called home on his cell phone, called the restaurant, called the apartment Cassie had lived in before she'd moved in with him.

Nothing. No answer at home or in her apartment. No message at the restaurant.

No Cassie.

Maybe, he thought as he strode into the terminal, maybe he'd figured wrong. Maybe she wasn't heading back to Vegas.

His gut told him she was. And it told him she was going to do it from this city's airport for no better reason than the name of the place itself.

Destiny. Fate. Providence.

He had nothing else to hang on to, except that.

Keir hurried through the terminal. It was crowded, but Cassie would be easy to see. She was tall. She was beautiful.

She was his heart.

But she wasn't there. He couldn't find her. Couldn't find her...

Will passenger Arlene Nevins please come to the Mid-Express ticket counter at gate four? Passenger Arlene Nevins...

Crowded, and noisy. The buzz of people. The announcements. One after another.

Passenger Edward Epstein, please come to the Trans-American counter at gate seven.

The announcements were driving him crazy. How could he concentrate with all those damned names floating around? If only it were that simple. If only he could ask someone to page Cassie...

Keir came to a sudden stop. A woman plowed into him and he muttered an apology, looked around and went to the nearest occupied gate.

"Excuse me," he said, pushing ahead of the people lined up at the counter, "sorry, but this is an emergency." The clerk looked up, annoyed, but Keir didn't give a damn. "I need to page someone."

"I'm sorry, sir. We don't do that."

"Of course you do. I've been listening to pages ever since I came through the door." He took a deep breath. You didn't get far, coming across as a crazy at an airline terminal these days. "Look, I have to find someone." He took another breath. "The woman I love is flying out of my life from this airport. You understand?"

The clerk's eyes flickered over Keir's face. "There's an information booth. You might try there."

Keir nodded, followed directions and faced another uniformed clerk five minutes later. He thought about what to say, decided to make it as brief as possible, and worked up a smile he hoped would make him look harmless.

"I have to locate someone. Can you page her for me?"

"For what reason, sir?"

Keir hesitated. Personal reasons? No. That could ring mental alarms. For love? That could ring alarms, too. He'd been stupid to tell that to the guy at the gate desk.

"Sir? For what reason?"

"The person in question works for me." Keir pulled an engraved business card from his pocket. He knew damn well it looked impressive. Raised black letters on a heavy vellum cream stock said, *Keir O'Connell, Owner. Deer Run Vineyard, Hamlin, Connecticut.*

The stony-faced clerk took the card and read it. He looked up, and, to Keir's relief, smiled.

"Mr. O'Connell. What a coincidence. My wife and I discovered your wines just a few weeks ago. We think they're wonderful."

"Great. Thanks. Keep the card. Come by for a visit. I'll

give you a tour and a private tasting. Look, about this page…"

"We tried your restaurant, too. Excellent food, sir. And excellent service."

"Yes, well, the lady I want paged manages that restaurant." Hurry up, Keir wanted to say, stop the chitchat and get to it. He smiled politely instead. "Why not bring your wife for dinner some evening? My compliments, Mr.…" He looked at the clerk's badge. "Mr. Conway. It would be our pleasure."

"Oh, that's very nice, Mr. O'Connell. We'd love to."

"Terrific." Keir scribbled a name on the back of another card. "Would you page this lady? Please?"

"Cassie Berk." The clerk looked up. "Is that correct?" At Keir's impatient, nod, Conway drew the microphone toward him, fiddled with it…

"Will passenger Cassie Berk come to the information desk? Passenger Cassie Berk. Come to the information desk, please." Conway switched off the mike. "That should do it, sir."

Keir nodded. "Yes," he said but he didn't believe it. Cassie would know he was the one paging her and she wouldn't respond.

She was here, though. He could sense her presence.

Minutes slipped by. No Cassie, even though the clerk repeated the announcement.

Cassie, Keir thought, pacing back and forth, Cassie, where are you? Why won't you come back to me? I love you, Cassandra. I love…

He swung toward the information desk. A woman was in earnest conversation with the clerk. Keir cleared his throat.

"Madam? I wonder if you'd mind letting me cut in here."

"I'm in a rush, young man."

"Yes, but I'm desperate. The woman I love is leaving me." To hell with how it sounded. If they decided he was a nutcase on the loose they'd drag him away, but it was worth the chance. "I have to page her and tell her I love her. I didn't, when I should have, and..." Keir took the woman's hand in his. "Please," he said.

The woman looked into his eyes. Then she smiled.

"Go on," she said softly, "and good luck."

Keir kissed her cheek, grabbed another card from his pocket and scribbled something on it. "Try this," he said, shoving the card at the clerk.

The clerk read what he'd written, looked up and frowned. "Cassandra Ber—ber—?"

"Cassandra Berk-oh-vitch," Keir said, pronouncing Cassie's name, *his* Cassie's name, with care. "Page her, please."

Cassie's name rang through the terminal. Once. Twice. Three times. And just when Keir was almost ready to admit defeat, he heard the whisper of her voice.

"Keir?"

He swung around and saw her, eyes glittering, mouth trembling.

He thought of all the things he wanted to tell here, but there was time for that. Years and years of time, if he was lucky. Right now, only the simplest words were important.

He had to say them.

She had to believe them.

Keir took a step toward her. "Cassandra," he said softly, "Cassandra, sweetheart. I love you."

The world seemed to stand still. He waited, heart pounding, and then she made a shaky sound that was half laugh, half sob.

"Keir. Keir, my love..."

Keir opened his arms. Cassie ran to him and he gathered her, forever, to his heart.

Cassandra Bercovic became Cassandra O'Connell in a simple ceremony that April at the Tender Grapes restaurant.

Dawn and Gray Baron flew in for the wedding.

"I'm so happy for you," Dawn told Cassie as they dressed that morning. "You're positively glowing."

Cassie smiled. "So are you. You're glow..." Dawn blushed, and Cassie's eyes widened. "Dawn! Are you pregnant?"

Dawn said yes, she was, and Cassie hugged her best friend and thought, not for the first time, how amazing and wonderful life could be.

Dawn was Cassie's matron of honor. Fallon, Megan and Briana were her bridesmaids. Gray was one of Keir's best men, along with Sean and Cullen.

The bridal planner had told them, solemnly, that it couldn't be done that way. You could only have one best man and if you had bridesmaids, then you needed a matching number of ushers.

"Is that a rule?" Keir had replied politely. "Because if it is, we'll be happy to break it."

The woman had looked from Keir to Cassie. A minute passed. Then her smile softened and she said she'd always wanted to help plan a wedding where the only thing that mattered was love.

After that, all the plans fell easily into place. Even the weather cooperated. The day of the wedding was exceptionally lovely and so warm that they took their vows on the terrace. Pots of yellow and red tulips sat on the little tables; they lined the aisle that had been marked off with streamers of red and yellow silk ribbon.

Cassie, wearing a long, old-fashioned gown of ivory French lace and a matching veil, carried a nosegay bouquet of spring flowers.

She was, her groom kept saying, beautiful.

She said he was beautiful, too, in his black tux.

Mary Elizabeth O'Connell Coyle agreed with them both, but as she told anyone who'd listen, what mattered more than the bride's beauty and the groom's good looks was the simple fact that the love they felt for each other shone in their eyes.

"Aren't they a lovely couple, Dan," she whispered to her husband.

Her smile was a bit wobbly but Dan understood that. This was the first of her children to wed.

"Lovely, darling," he whispered back, and slipped his arm around her shoulders.

Cassie's matron of honor sniffled into her hanky all through the ceremony. Her sisters-in-law, who all adored her, sniffled, too. Well, all except Fallon, who watched with the kind of pleasant curiosity anthropologists afford native ceremonies.

Sean and Cullen, who were crazy about their new sister-in-law, shot Keir blinding smiles, then looked at each other, rolled their eyes and silently vowed such an awful thing as marriage would never happen to them. Gray reached for his wife's hand and brought it to his lips.

Keir and Cassie noticed none of it.

They never took their eyes from each other. When the justice of the peace pronounced them man and wife they went into each other's arms and exchanged a kiss so long, so tender, so filled with promise that the assembled guests applauded.

Some of the women wept.

Even Fallon felt a dampness on her lashes.

Surely, she thought, blinking as she looked up into the blue, cloudless sky, surely, what she'd felt was only rain.

The world's bestselling romance series.

HARLEQUIN®
Presents

Seduction and Passion Guaranteed!

GREEK TYCOONS

They're the men who have everything—
except a bride...

Wealth, power, charm—what else could a heart-stopping handsome tycoon need? Find out in the GREEK TYCOONS miniseries, where your very favorite authors introduce gorgeous Greek multimillionaires who are in need of wives!

Coming soon in Harlequin Presents®

SMOKESCREEN MARRIAGE by Sara Craven
#2320, on sale May 2003

THE GREEK TYCOON'S BRIDE by Helen Brooks
#2328, on sale June 2003

THE GREEK'S SECRET PASSION by Sharon Kendrick
#2339, on sale August 2003

Available wherever Harlequin books are sold.

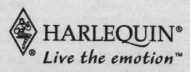

HARLEQUIN®
Live the emotion™

Visit us at www.eHarlequin.com

HPGTYC

If you enjoyed what you just read,
then we've got an offer you can't resist!

Take 2 bestselling
love stories FREE!

Plus get a FREE surprise gift!

Clip this page and mail it to Harlequin Reader Service®

IN U.S.A.	IN CANADA
3010 Walden Ave.	P.O. Box 609
P.O. Box 1867	Fort Erie, Ontario
Buffalo, N.Y. 14240-1867	L2A 5X3

YES! Please send me 2 free Harlequin Presents® novels and my free surprise gift. After receiving them, if I don't wish to receive anymore, I can return the shipping statement marked cancel. If I don't cancel, I will receive 6 brand-new novels every month, before they're available in stores! In the U.S.A., bill me at the bargain price of $3.57 plus 25¢ shipping & handling per book and applicable sales tax, if any*. In Canada, bill me at the bargain price of $4.24 plus 25¢ shipping & handling per book and applicable taxes**. That's the complete price and a savings of at least 10% off the cover prices—what a great deal! I understand that accepting the 2 free books and gift places me under no obligation ever to buy any books. I can always return a shipment and cancel at any time. Even if I never buy another book from Harlequin, the 2 free books and gift are mine to keep forever.

106 HDN DNTZ
306 HDN DNT2

Name	(PLEASE PRINT)	
Address	Apt.#	
City	State/Prov.	Zip/Postal Code

 * Terms and prices subject to change without notice. Sales tax applicable in N.Y.
** Canadian residents will be charged applicable provincial taxes and GST.
   All orders subject to approval. Offer limited to one per household and not valid to
   current Harlequin Presents® subscribers.
   ® are registered trademarks of Harlequin Enterprises Limited.

PRES02   ©2001 Harlequin Enterprises Limited

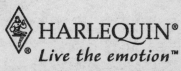

The world's bestselling romance series.

HARLEQUIN®
Presents

Seduction and Passion Guaranteed!

VIVA LA VIDA DE AMOR!

They speak the language of passion.

In Harlequin Presents®, you'll find a special kind of lover—full of Latin charm. Whether he's relaxing in denims, or dressed for dinner, giving you diamonds, or simply sweet dreams, he's got spirit, style and sex appeal!

Look out for our next Latin Lovers titles:

A SPANISH INHERITANCE by Susan Stephens
#2318, on sale April 2003

ALEJANDRO'S REVENGE by Anne Mather
#2327, on sale June 2003

Available wherever Harlequin books are sold.

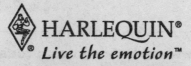

HARLEQUIN®
Live the emotion™

Visit us at www.eHarlequin.com

HPLATMAR